POPSICLE STYX

POPSICLE STYX

John T. Biggs

P
Pen-L Publishing
Fayetteville, AR
Pen-L.com

I

"Double stick orange today." The H-Unit guard puts down his red and white insulated cooler and shakes hands with the Reverend Richard Harjo. "Strawberry tomorrow. Grape the day after."

Richard knows the routine. Death row inmates get popsicles when the air conditioning can't keep pace with summer. June, July, and August. Sometimes the first week in September.

"Name's Anton Leemaster." The guard points to his nametag. "Just transferred in from visitation."

Richard doesn't bother to look. The inmate population in H-Unit changes slowly but guards are shifted on a regular schedule so they won't bond with the men—and one woman—whose cells are nearest to the death chamber.

Some prisoners get friendly when their execution day is close. The dozen inmates in this small section of H-Unit have the shortest time. Next vacancy in two days. Then it's Moving Day again. It's Richard Harjo's job to ease the minds of people who know the exact minute they're going to die. Put them on speaking terms with God—whoever that is. Calm them down so they don't make a scene when the time comes to slide the needle into a vein. If his Doctorate of Divinity doesn't do the trick, his PhD in psychology probably will. If he screws it up there'll be no one to complain—in this world anyway—and meantime there are orange popsicles.

Three H-Unit residents are on the docket for the month of August. That's some kind of record. Richard counts them on his fingers. Whispers names without meaning to, "Tammy Wynette Biggerstaff, Oba Leon Taylor, Holabi Minco."

The guard smiles and nods his head after each one. "Oklahoma's gonna beat Texas this month for sure." He gives Richard a nervous laugh. Turns it into a cough to show there's nothing funny about H-Unit. Where people are strapped onto a gurney. Where they are injected with a lethal combination of drugs with the push of a button by three executioners who enter and leave the building wearing black hoods. Like actors in a movie about the Spanish Inquisition.

"Take a popsicle, Reverend." The guard opens his cooler. "Hell, take two. Give one to Mr. Minco when you pass his cell." The guard stares at the steel door of Holabi Minco's cell.

"It'll be a good day when that one's gone." Anton Leemaster holds the cooler so Richard can take his pick.

"He's been on H-Unit for three years," Richard Harjo says. "Death row short-timer."

Holabi had waved off the Civil Liberties Union and the Coalition to Abolish the Death Penalty. Didn't request a new court appointed attorney. Hadn't written letters to the governor. Hadn't asked Chaplain Richard Harjo to pray with him either. Now that he's so close, maybe he'll change his mind.

"Popsicle's a good way for a holy man to break the ice with a witchy Indian," Anton Leemaster says. Another nervous laugh. "He eats one every day, they tell me." He nods at Holabi Minco's cell as the inmate's face appears behind the window in the steel door that separates him from the civilized world.

The prisoner stretches his lips around two fingers and gives a shill whistle through the slotted speaking vent. "Come on over, Rev. I won't bite."

Well, maybe he will and maybe he won't. It's too late to think about it. Richard Harjo is already moving toward the cell like a faithful hunting dog.

"Harjo's a Creek name, ain't it?" Holabi Minco pokes one hand out the pass-through where prisoners receive meals, books and letters. He takes his orange popsicle without breaking eye contact. He peels the wrapper off, wads it into a tight ball and tosses it out the pass-through. He bites off half of the orange ice and swallows it without chewing.

"Creek and Choctaw are cousins, Rev." He takes another giant bite. Chews this one. Says, "Stop by and see me when you're done with Tammy."

Before Richard can ask how Holabi knows his schedule, the inmate tells him. "She's next to go. Naturally she'll want to see a holy man."

Holy man? Richard's been called that twice today, another H-Unit record.

"Tammy's a cute little redhead, Rev, but she's real dangerous. That girl's an old-school man killer." Minco makes a smooching sound with his lips.

"One way or the other she'll leave her mark on you." The inmate crushes the remains of his popsicle in his hand and draws four orange lines across the viewing window. "See if I ain't right."

2

"I ain't done nothing wrong. Those boys needed killin.'" Tammy Wynette Biggerstaff gives Richard Harjo the same explanation she gave her jury when she took the stand against her attorney's advice seven years ago. It hadn't convinced them and it doesn't convince the chaplain as he sits beside her on the cement bunk that cantilevers from the wall of her death row cell.

Tammy shakes her head so her red hair falls over her shoulders like an erotic sculpture made of copper wire. Richard tries to find a neutral place to settle his eyes, but they follow their own testosterone agenda. They explore every inch of Tammy Biggerstaff. She notices, of course.

She scoots closer—something Richard doesn't expect. She licks the drops off her orange popsicle with the tip of her tongue, puts the double-tip into her mouth and draws the sugary liquid into her mouth until the color fades from sunset orange to a dull pastel. Cute and dangerous. An old-school man killer, like Holabi Minco said.

Richard feels like she's pulled all the air out of the room. He can't get enough oxygen breathing at the normal rate, or at twice the normal rate. He recognizes the symptoms of a panic attack. It's happened before. Understandable when he's alone in a cell with a murderer. Nobody watching him but Jesus, and Richard hasn't been sure of Jesus for quite some time.

Tammy smiles. It's hard to believe such a little girl killed three teenage boys. Killed them with a knife. Mutilated them. Probably smiled when she did it, exactly the way she's smiling at Richard Harjo. His hands and feet begin to cramp—early signs of hyperventilation. His visual field turns black around the edges so it looks like Tammy Wynette Biggerstaff is at the far end of a long tunnel.

When he thinks of her that way he feels better. Far, far, away. Much too far to reach out and touch him on the leg—the way she's doing now. He feels the heat from her body radiating through her powder blue jumpsuit with OK DOC stenciled across the front and back. She fills that suit out nicely, even through his hyperoxic haze. Richard knows he won't be able to stop thinking about Tammy even when he leaves her cell. He needs to do that pretty soon before he passes out.

"Maybe we should pray," he says.

She talks right through his suggestion. Fast, like a television background voice reciting the side effects of a brand new wonder drug. Richard can understand little of what she's saying. Mostly he's thinking about her brilliant red hair that he'd like to run his fingers through, and the spray of freckles across her cheeks that make her look about twelve years old, and the chip in a central incisor that offsets the perfect symmetry of her face. He wonders which one of her delicate hands held the knife that took the lives of three young, strong boys who, "needed killin.'" Tammy Wynette Biggerstaff's eyes are the color of early spring when everything in Oklahoma starts to bloom and storms blow out of the west, full of moisture and electricity.

"Tammy . . . ." Richard interrupts her monologue. Wants to tell her everything will be all right, but he's never been good at lying.

"Yes?" Her breath smells like marshmallows floating in hot chocolate, and Richard Harjo has an awful craving.

When he doesn't say anything more, Tammy stands. She paces around the tiny cell that's taller than it is long or wide. She doesn't get too far away—that would be impossible—but far enough that Richard can see how small she is.

Maybe ninety pounds.

"Soaking wet," he says without meaning to. "Sorry. Don't know where that came from."

But Tammy Wynette Biggerstaff is talking non-stop again. She shoots words into the room rapid fire. She tells Richard Harjo about her stepfather,

Burdette Lafleur, who, "gave me naked whupins with his belt." She covers her bottom with both hands. Looks at Richard Harjo. Measures his reaction.

He smiles, even though that doesn't seem like the right thing to do.

"He let Wolfie watch," she says. "My stepbrother, you know. And after the whupins, sometimes they'd . . . ."

Richard Harjo knows exactly what they'd do, even if Tammy Wynette Biggerstaff won't say. He can picture it perfectly in his mind. Wishes he couldn't. He's repulsed by the mental image. Titillated by it too. Just a little, but enough so that he can't get that image out of his mind. Especially when Tammy sits down beside him again and puts her arms around him and cries onto his shoulder. What is it about a pretty woman's tears?

"I really think it's time to pray," Richard Harjo says. "Let's close our eyes." So she won't see the erection he hopes will go away when he gets a direct line to Jesus.

"Dear God . . . ." Nothing original comes to mind so he plagiarizes John 3:16. Tammy kisses him on the cheek when he says, "Amen."

There's no lipstick permitted on death row. Something to be thankful for.

3

Richard Harjo looks into the window of Holabi Minco's cell. The prisoner is sitting on his cement bunk arranging popsicle sticks in parallel rows. He looks up as Richard is about to walk away.

A man's voice from down the hall says, "He wants to see you, Reverend."

Anton Leemaster? The other male guard? Richard can't be sure. There are three regulars for every death row shift. Three guards who accompany condemned inmates to the underground exercise yard where they walk in shackles for an hour a day while custodial specialists clean and search their cells for contraband. Two male guards and one female—since Tammy Wynette Biggerstaff came into the unit. A woman jailer, so Tammy will feel more comfortable when they take her to the shower, or the medical clinic where they'll verify she's healthy enough to execute at 6:02 a.m. Sunday morning. Two days from now.

"Whenever anyone looks into Minco's cell, he always looks back." It's Leemaster all right. He stands too close to Richard. Crowding his personal space the way Tammy Biggerstaff did.

"Like a damn cat. Nobody can sneak up on that one." Leemaster fumbles with a set of complicated mechanical keys. Primitive and reliable. In the general population everything is electronic. Not in H-Unit. Condemned prisoners are too dangerous for the fickle nature of electrons.

Anton Leemaster shouts, "Stand away from the door, Minco."

Two more sets of footsteps close in behind Richard Harjo. A triangle of guards. The new arrivals are armed with truncheons—all according to regulations. They don't follow regulations with every inmate, but with Minco they do.

"He's a witchy one," Leemaster says. "Whole damn family's witchy."

Based on rumors, Richard knows. The oral history of the penitentiary tribe. Everybody accepts the stories as fact. The more unbelievable they are, the more everyone believes them. According to Department of Corrections legends, Choctaw spirits kill people at Holabi Minco's bidding. He can look into a man's eyes and take control of his soul. He can turn into an owl and fly to the land of the dead where nothing can be kept from him. Like an Old Testament Fallen Angel.

The inmate walks to the wall opposite his cell door. Places his hands against it in the classical arrest posture.

"Careful, Reverend," the female guard tells Richard. "My people say this one's got powers."

My people. Richard's grandmother talked that way. My people. Our people. The people—as if they were the only ones who mattered. Grandma Clementine Harjo was an old-time Indian. Mixed her English with Muscogee Creek. Raised her orphaned grandson on a blend of Native American Mythology and Christianity. Not really all that different, as far as Richard can see.

"Thanks for the warning." He doesn't have to look at the female guard to know she'll have long black hair stuffed under her uniform cap. She'll have the dark eyes and bronze skin that go with Native American blood. Almost everybody in this part of Oklahoma has a little. Many of the prison guards and most of the inmates have a lot.

"Come on in, Rev," Holabi Minco calls over his shoulder. "I ain't got much time left. Don't want to spend it standing by a prison toilet."

Minco stays in position until the door is locked. Richard turns and looks at the viewing window. All he can see is the reflection of the overhead fluorescent lights.

"Squint your eyes," Minco says. "Helps to see faces through the glare."

The female guard on the other side of the reinforced glass is dividing her attention equally between the chaplain and the inmate.

Minco points at his cement bunk. "Take a load off, preacher. Madeline will get bored after she sees nothin's gonna happen."

Madeline. Now Richard knows the names of two H-Unit guards.

"Knew her from when she was a little girl. Friend of the family you might say. A magic man needs lots of friends, Rev." Holabi sits on his bunk. Lays down a long row popsicle sticks like rungs in a ladder spanning the distance between him and Richard Harjo. Names are written on three sticks: Tammy Wynette Biggerstaff, Oba Leon Taylor, Lorado Lopez.

"Stick calendar," Holabi says. "Choctaw kept track of time on a big long stick before we got all civilized. This here's the death row version." He walks the fingers of his right hand down the center of his row of popsicle sticks. "This here's the month of August—Women's Month, my people call it. Laid out to gage the time between executions."

Richard wants to ask, Where's your stick, Holabi? Instead he says, "Lorado Lopez isn't scheduled. He's got an appeal still pending." Richard had stopped by Lorado's cell a time or two since he moved to the row, but the murderer hadn't been in a visitation frame of mind.

"You got family, Rev? Momma or a Papa Harjo?" Holabi looks at Richard. Shakes his head. "I guess you don't."

Prison rules say not to talk about your personal life with inmates. Especially murderers, but Richard's family has been dead for years so it can't possibly matter. "Raised by my Grandma Clementine. Mom and Dad passed over when I was a boy."

Passed over. Sounds peaceful, but it wasn't—not for either of them. Richard doesn't tell Holabi Minco how his parents died. He hasn't told anyone since he took the job as H-Unit chaplain. Probably wouldn't have gotten the job if they knew.

"Clementine." Richard hasn't said the name out loud for quite some time. It catches in his throat. "How about you, Minco? Got anybody?"

The death row inmate checks Richard Harjo out, head to toe. Lingers on his face long enough to count his eyelashes. Minco moves his lips without making a sound, as if he's weighing pros and cons before coming to an important decision.

"I'd rather you were Choctaw, Rev. Even Chickasaw, but I guess a Creek will have to do." Minco scoops up the three bottom sticks, two blanks and one with Tammy Wynette Biggerstaff's name on it. He puts them into Richard's shirt pocket.

"Little gift, Rev. Maybe you'll bring me something in return."

Richard starts to tell him that's not allowed, but Minco holds a hand up like a traffic cop.

"Quid pro quo," Holabi Minco says. "Latin makes everything sound legal, don't it, Rev? Latin ain't as magic as Choctaw, but pretty close."

The three Latin words wouldn't be much of an excuse if one of the guards reported Richard for taking things from Holabi Minco. Or bringing things to the inmate. That would be worse. That would be a class D felony. A fine. Maybe jail time. He'd definitely lose his job.

"You've been on the row for three years now," Richard says. "You don't seem like you're afraid."

Holabi shrugs. He finger thumps the sticks in Richard pocket. It makes the Chaplain's heart skip a beat.

"So why'd you suddenly want to talk to me?"

"Tried to work it out another way, Rev," Holabi says. "Thought maybe I wouldn't need a holy man, but I do."

Richard waits for Minco to ask him about Jesus, and Heaven, and whether a murderer has a chance of getting past the bouncer at the Pearly Gates, but the inmate doesn't have any of the usual questions. He doesn't have any questions at all.

"It'll all come clear in the end, Rev. Ain't that what bein' a holy man's all about?"

My people say this one's got powers. Richard's pretty sure Grandma Clementine would agree with Madeline one hundred percent.

4

Richard Harjo removes the popsicle sticks from his shirt pocket. He lays them out on his kitchen table the way Holabi Minco arranged them on his bunk. There's something else in his pocket he hadn't noticed. A feather, as long as his middle finger. Put there by Minco, Richard is sure of it. A sleight of hand trick by a murderer who wants everyone to believe he's a sorcerer.

The feather is too large to belong to a wren or sparrow. Wrong shape and color pattern for an eagle—alternating brown and white stripes, arranged like rungs on a ladder.

Or a popsicle stick calendar.

The vane of the feather feels slick, as if it's coated with a film of oil. A tingling sensation begins in Richard Harjo's fingertips and spreads to his wrist—a numb, dead feeling.

Owl feather. He doesn't have to Google an Audubon website to identify it. Owls are key figures in the dark side of Native American mysticism. Eagles brush their wings against Heaven and Owls brush theirs against . . . .

Richard says, "the opposite of Heaven," out loud before he can stop himself. He looks around the kitchen, reassures himself that no one is present to witness his surrender to magical ideation. People with PhDs in psychology don't believe in things like Heaven and Hell and magic feathers.

But a Doctor of Divinity might. If the conditions are right. If he's spent time with a woman who will die at 6:02 Sunday morning and a murderer who could be a Choctaw witch.

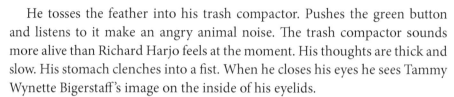

He tosses the feather into his trash compactor. Pushes the green button and listens to it make an angry animal noise. The trash compactor sounds more alive than Richard Harjo feels at the moment. His thoughts are thick and slow. His stomach clenches into a fist. When he closes his eyes he sees Tammy Wynette Bigerstaff's image on the inside of his eyelids.

Cute and dangerous.

Something pops inside the trash compactor and her image disappears.

Tomorrow he'll visit her again. Pray with her. Pretend there's something waiting for her on the other side. Right now all he wants to do is sleep. Every day's a long one on H-Unit when three executions are scheduled in a month.

"Maybe the governor will call," he tells the popsicle stick with Tammy's name written on it in neat looping red letters, the kind of handwriting nuns used to teach in Catholic School. Is Holabi Minco Catholic? Richard doesn't think so. Not enough guilt in his eyes. Not enough respect in his voice.

The Reverend straightens the popsicle sticks so they are perfectly parallel. So there's exactly the same amount of space between the rungs on the stick calendar. Tomorrow they'll move Tammy into the cell next to the death chamber. A technician will check her veins—find the best one for when the time comes. She'll have her last shower. Select her last meal—no alcohol, nothing from further away than fifteen miles, nothing over fifteen dollars. She'll hear a lot of noes and nothings. The most important "no" will come after she asks if there's any word from the governor.

The death row chaplain's job is to offer Tammy Biggerstaff the hope of Heaven, which is the only hope she really has, because in all the years since Oklahoma became a state, no governor has ever called.

Richard Harjo lies in his bed thinking of all the terrible people who still believe in the power of prayer. Thieves, con men, rapists, and murderers ask for absolution, promise to sin no more—an easy promise because committing their kind of sins takes Herculean effort inside an H-Unit prison cell.

Creek grandmothers believe in prayer too. The power of favors asked to a Middle-Eastern God with an appetite for European rituals. Richard tries to remember the exact date when he stopped asking God for personal favors. He still goes through the motions when he's on the job. Still pretends, during prison services. Tries to convince inmates that Heaven is a supernatural work-release program and Jesus is the most gullible probation officer ever.

Is there a special place in Hell for hypocrite ministers? Does Hell exist? Does Heaven? There are smart men who believe they do, but none of them are scientists. Richard has studied the chemistry and biology of faith. The interactions of norepinephrine and serotonin combined with misfires in the brain that account for everything.

Dr. Richard Harjo, PhD, tells himself prayer is meaningless, but Reverend Richard Harjo thinks it might be worth another try.

"Dear God . . . ." He starts off in the usual way. Eyes closed. Voice dripping with fake sincerity. As if he could put one over on The Man Who Made The World—that's what Grandma Clementine called The Creator.

"Dear Man Who Made The World . . . ." Changing the name doesn't help.

Faith is believing in something you can only see if your eyes are closed. It's dark in Richard's bedroom but he squeezes his eyelids together anyway. A few sparks of light flash across his retinas but they don't gather into the face of Jesus.

"Amen." Reverend Richard Harjo gives his incomplete prayer a proper ending in case there's someone—or something—out there listening.

Grandma Clementine would blame his crises of faith on his PhD. "Educated people think they're too smart to believe in God," she told him. She was right, but knowing that doesn't help Richard Harjo now.

It's not a good time to think troubling thoughts when your head is on a pillow and the lights are out. Not the right time at all, but Richard's mind keeps coming back to the notion of Heaven and Hell and hypocrisy until the random sparks of light on his retinas organize themselves into a dream.

Tammy Wynette Biggerstaff isn't wearing her powder blue jump suit anymore. She's not in her tiny cement death row cell. And she's not alone.

Tammy Biggerstaff is naked on an iron four-poster bed with a sagging mattress and noisy springs doing things with another woman that Reverend Harjo would say are sinful, but Doctor Harjo, PhD, finds fascinating.

A tramp stamp traces a scalloped pattern at the top of Tammy's buttocks. Richard wants to look away but can't. A bright blue tattooed butterfly ripples over her right shoulder blade as Tammy loses herself in a sensual rhythm on top of a muscular woman with a mullet haircut.

Tammy moans, "Samantha," in a voice that sounds as if it's been drowned in expensive whisky.

Richard doesn't understand the mechanics of what the two women are doing but he appreciates the choreography. They roll from one edge of the bed to the other, like a pair of professional wrestlers who know exactly how this match will turn out in the end. Perfectly staged as if they know someone is watching. Every move has been rehearsed for maximum effect just in case the spirit of Richard Harjo happens to be floating near the ceiling, watching everything.

Floating feels perfectly natural, the way impossible things always do in dreams.

The two women take turns pinning each other. There is scratching and pinching, a couple of loud spanks. They moan like a pair of cats in heat. Panthers, who care everything about ecstasy and nothing for reproduction.

The vocalizations reach their peak when Tammy and her girlfriend have simultaneous orgasms. Richard has seen things like that on pay per view pornography during hour and twenty minute periods of moral weakness. He never imagined they had a basis in reality. Thought it was like walking on water, and virgin births, and images of Jesus on whole wheat toast. Something hatched out in fertile erotic minds, performed by skilled X-rated actors like Linda Lovelace, Marilyn Chambers and Harry Reems.

When the acrobatics are finished, Tammy Wynette Biggerstaff sits up in the bed. She clutches her arms around her breasts. Leans forward so Richard can read the name, Samantha, printed along the top of her trapezius muscle in flamboyant black calligraphy.

She cries, the way she cried on Richard's shoulder in her cell. But her lover doesn't respond the way Richard did. She doesn't say a prayer and pretend she's not turned on.

Samantha says, "Cool it, Tammy." She stands, and turns her back on Tammy Wynette Biggerstaff. "You're such a drama queen."

Richard doesn't think Samantha knows about the three boys Tammy killed. Or maybe she hasn't killed them yet. This dream is in the past. He can't be sure how long ago.

It really doesn't matter because Tammy has the knife. The knife she used—or will use—to kill and mutilate three boys with lean masculine bodies and butch ideas about young women that are not much different from Samantha's.

Tammy's lover tips her head backward, looks directly into Richard Harjo's eyes.

Richard hovers above her like an owl feather floating on an Oklahoma breeze.

Samantha places her right hand above her eyes as if she's a soldier saluting a superior officer. She squints her eyes at Richard, the way he squinted his in Holabi Minco's prison cell so he could see a face behind the reflection in the one and only window.

"What the fu . . . ." Samantha's voice starts off full of confidence but finishes full of blood.

Tammy is behind her, shorter than Samantha, weaker than Samantha, but more dangerous than Samantha, because she has a knife in her hand. Something she always keeps close at hand just in case Burdette and Wolfie Lafleur come for her again.

She screams and plunges the blade between Samantha's ribs. Pulls it free. Finds another target. Strikes again.

After the second stroke Samantha turns and faces Tammy. Bloody bubbles pop between her lips. She coughs bright red splatters onto Tammy's face. They are lost among her freckles.

"Samantha?" Tammy looks surprised to see the face of her lover on the body she's just stabbed.

"You're so much like him from behind," Tammy says. "Like Wolfie, you know? Everybody who loves me looks like Wolfie from behind."

Samantha falls onto her knees. The way James Brown—the hardest working man in show business—ended rhythm and blues songs with a choreographed collapse.

But Samantha's collapse isn't choreographed. She looks up at Tammy through eyes that are already starting to glaze over and says, "Floating man."

Richard thinks that couldn't be right, but she says, "Floating man," once more, as clear and meaningless as a confession to a priest, before she collapses on the bedroom floor. As last words go, he supposes they are as good as any.

5

The sign over Nasty's Titty Bar leaves nothing to Wolfie Lafleur's imagination. Photo realistic Indian girls with their legs wrapped around brass poles and expressions on their faces that promise an orgasm is only a lap dance away.

Going inside is out of the question. Too many Injun-cowboys in this bar. Most of them are strapped with old time revolvers. There'd be trouble if they got a look at the white power tattoos on his biceps. He could cover the ink with long sleeves but only junkies wear long sleeves in August, and even mud-race strippers don't approve of junkies.

Neither do half-breed cowboys who've drunk most of their paychecks and stuffed the rest into G-strings. The mud races are such judgmental assholes. They don't appreciate the fact that Wolfie is doing them a favor. That he's come here to share some DNA from one of the twelve truly chosen tribes.

Of course he needs to get laid too. It's been slim pickings since his half sister went to prison.

He backs his red Chevy Silverado into a parking place between two Ford Rangers that are splotched with bondo and gray primer. He kills the engine, but leaves his key in the ignition so he's ready for a quick escape.

If he gets lucky, that is. And Wolfie is almost sure to get lucky pretty soon. It's two a.m., which means the first shift girls are ready to come out—the ones who haven't hooked up for private dances—and the second shift girls will be showing up for work. The dancers park at the far end of the lot so the drunks leaving the club don't ding up their paint and the sober incoming customers won't waste their energy on a long walk to the front door. Wolfie's truck is at the border of the customer zone. Far enough from the club so nobody will hear anything if his girl screams. Close enough so he can check his target in the light from the sign.

Wolfie's hoping to catch a fresh one driving in from Daisy or Jumbo, but mud-race girls are never all that fresh and he's really not particular as long as she's got all her front teeth.

He rolls his windows down and listens to the music inside the bar. Something with a lot of bass. He doesn't recognize the song but he recognizes the beat. It's like the pounding of his heart when ecstasy kicks in. He holds a tab in his hand, and checks his watch. He lets the second hand make a complete circuit. He doesn't pop the pill into his mouth until a full minute passes, as a show of self-control.

Self-control is what being a member of the master race is all about. It says that in the Bible—so he's been told— in the book with all the begets. The Book of Geniuses. He remembers that from the last time his dad preached at a Christian Identity service. Wolfie's brain is pretty good—not like people say—even if the part he uses to read is missing a transistor or two.

He pops another ecstasy and waits for the world to start looking rosier. He feels the change coming over him even before the pills have made their way down his esophagus.

Placebo effect, scientists call it. That rhymes with *spasibo*, which means thank you in Russian. Who needs reading when you can watch the Discovery Channel on TV?

Wolfie can read some things, of course. Things like Nasty's Titty Bar. Strong words hang on to their place in line. Letters freeze solid and don't jump around if they've got a little nasty-glue holding them together.

"Dyslexia," a Jew high school counselor explained the learning disability to him before he spit in her face. Some folks are born with it. Some have it knocked into their heads by their daddies. Reading is mostly a waste of time anyway.

Wolfie is a really smart man, even if he can't read. He knows how to get money, and food, and ecstasy, and all the muddy girls a white boy could ever want. And he knows about alibis and reasonable doubt and the right to remain silent. Stuff from lawyer shows on the USA channel.

One of the stripper girls walks out of the bar. Wolfie strains to see if she's wearing a bra under her T-shirt but the light from the sign isn't good enough. The girls all wear jeans outside the club. Faded ones usually with holes in the knees. Their pockets bulge with five-dollar bills. This one scans the parking lot before she steps out of the bouncer's protective zone.

"G'night Bruce." She gives the big no-neck monster in the doorway a little finger wave. Smiles like she might let him in her pants.

Wolfie knows that's just a flirtation. The bouncer is big and brawny but he has a gay name. That and the way he moves is a dead giveaway.

The ecstasy is already making Wolfie sweat. His eyes dilate so it looks like somebody turned up wattage on titty bar sign. The muddy girl slinks past him across the parking lot, moving her ass in time to the base notes that have made it through the club's frame walls.

Whoring comes natural to the muddy girls. They'll sit in your lap for twenty dollars. Grind their asses into your crotch the way a meth cook grinds crystals with a mortar and a pestle. Then when you're all worked up they hop off and ask for fifty more, "For a private session. You know . . . a private session," in the back room where Bruce the gay bouncer never goes.

The stripper's little butt slides back and forth drawing perfect figure eights. She has a gap between her legs. Skinny girl. Pretty girl. Muddy girl.

"Hey there, baby."

She smiles at him—they always do that when things start off. They smile because they think Wolfie might be a customer and they wouldn't want to offend a regular even though they don't bother putting names with faces in Nasty's Titty Bar.

She smiles, but she holds her car key in her clenched fist so the part that sticks into the ignition protrudes between her fingers. That won't do her any good. Wolfie has a secret weapon. Something he stole from Animal Control in Muskogee, Oklahoma.

He has a pellet rifle all pumped up and loaded with a dart. And when the muddy girl is past him, working her behind a little more because she thinks she's out of reach, he shoots that ass.

One shot is all he gets. One dart loaded with enough ketamine to stop her in her tracks. Similar to angel dust, Wolfie's been told, if you inject a line dose. Enough drug to gork the brain but not enough to slide it into the K-hole of general anesthesia.

She jumps when the dart hits her ass. As if she's been slapped. Wolfie knows that happens a lot in titty bars. Nipples get pinched. Bottoms get spanked. Hickeys are left in places that are sure to have a bad effect on tips.

Ketamine works super fast. She stumbles a little. Drops her keys. Pulls the dart out of her ass and looks at it like it's the most interesting thing in the world. By the time she figures out she's been tranqued, Wolfie is standing beside her. Turning on the charm.

"What's your name, sweetheart?" Ketamine doesn't turn muscles into mush. The girl can still walk if she's nudged along. She hardly notices she's being wrangled to his truck. She's lost track of concepts like dark nights, and dangerous perverts waiting in ambush.

"What's your name?" He asks again. Sometimes it takes a while for language to penetrate the K-barrier.

"Linda?" She asks. Thinks about it while she stumbles toward Wolfie's car.

"Linda Sanchez," she says. "Definitely Linda Sanchez."

Hispanic. This is Wolfie's lucky day. Mexicans are the least muddy of the second-class races. He eases her into the front seat of his car and fastens the seatbelt around her. Ecstasy has dried out his mouth and made it hard to swallow. His heart rate has passed the residential speed limit.

Linda Sanchez is prettier than most strippers. She'll be even prettier when he wipes the whore makeup off her face and throws her into the shower. Can't wash the mud away but Linda Sanchez is in the middle of a ketamine flop sweat and she smells a little ripe. Nothing that can't be fixed with Ivory soap.

"Ninety-nine and forty-four one hundredths pure," he tells her.

Linda Sanchez tries for a smile but only one side of her face cooperates.

"How you doin', Linda? Feeling gnarly?"

"Linda Sanchez?" She doesn't try to smile this time. Doesn't even look his way. She sinks deeper into the K-hole. Deep enough for surgery or pornography or rape. She'll only stay that way for twenty minutes unless Wolfie injects her again. He secures her hands and ankles with plastic ties so she won't be too much trouble if she comes out of it before he reaches his hideaway in the Jack Fork Mountains, in the forest just beyond the Patch.

It's a weird little place, not big enough to be a town. People of all kinds live there: blacks, Mexicans, Indians, whites too—mostly white at least. Patch people all have one thing in common. They mind their own business. They won't interfere if Linda screams while he's driving down the secret dirt road that leads though the place that's not on Google Maps.

He reaches over and tips Linda's head back. Opens up her airway so she won't suffocate before he gets a chance at her. Won't matter so much if she dies after—or even during.

"Rather put a baby inside you if I can." He thumps her on the head with his index finger. It makes a sound like a ripe watermelon. "But in the end, it don't really matter, Linda. It don't matter much at all."

"This ain't my first rodeo mister." Linda Sanchez no longer has that Special K look in her eyes. She doesn't squirm like Wolfie hoped she would. Doesn't whimper and make promises. Doesn't put up any struggle when he drags her out of the truck and makes her hop all the way to the cabin door.

"You oughta at least uncinch my feet," she says. "You've got to sooner or later, don't you?"

Wolfie doesn't like tough girls. He shoves her through the front door, not quite hard enough to send her sprawling on her face. That brings a little squeak to the back of her throat. It's a start.

"Won't do no good to scream." He unfastens the plastic cinches and starts undressing her. The T-shirt first. Just like he'd hoped, no bra underneath. No panties under the jeans either. That's even better than a thong. He'll let her keep the ones and fives in her pockets. Wolfie Lafleur is no thief.

He puts himself between the stripper and the door so she won't try to run away. Sometimes they cover up. Pretend they haven't been groped and ogled by a thousand half-breed cowboys. Not Linda Sanchez. She crosses her arms underneath her breasts so her nipples point at him like a double barrel shotgun.

"Go on," she says. "Do what you have to do, and then let me go. I'd appreciate it if you didn't leave no bruises I can't cover with concealer."

Wolfie pushes her into the bathroom. Tells her it's time for a shower. "Like my women clean," he says.

And scared, he doesn't say. And just a little muddy.

Does she know about the chosen tribes and the mud races? Does she know she doesn't have a soul? No more than a rabbit or a squirrel? That's what Wolfie's dad told him. Ain't a sin to kill mud people. Like fumigating roaches or putting flea powder on a dog.

Wolfie doesn't plan to kill this one. Not that he couldn't have a change of plans. He'll fill her up with half-white babies and then set her free in the woods to make her way back home as best she can. People from the Patch might take her in for a while, if their watchdogs don't get her first.

Patch folk don't care for rape, but they like policemen even less. They'll feed Linda Sanchez. They'll clean her up and give her a ride to the turnpike and explain how going to the cops doesn't make sense for a girl like her.

Cops don't investigate crimes that happen in the Jack Fork Mountains. Cops pretend this part of the world ain't really here.

"Best to let bygones be bygones," Wolfie says out loud—as if he lived in the Patch and is accustomed to cleaning up after white supremacist rapists.

"What'd you say?" Linda Sanchez washes off the Injun-cowboy fingerprints, and the chewing tobacco slobbers and the film of second hand smoke that makes her smell like a used ashtray.

Not many tats. Wolfie likes girls without much ink. A yellow butterfly on her left butt cheek, a heart with some initials on her right breast, and a tasteful rose on one ankle.

"Tasteful Rose." Wolfie pops another ecstasy, even though the first two are still on line. The peak is passed, so it probably won't make him sick. His temperature is already cooling down. His salivary glands are back in business.

"Re-opened under new management." There's no way Linda Sanchez could know Wolfie's talking about saliva, so the look she gives him is no surprise.

"Waxing poetic," he tells her. Words just slip out of Wolfie when he's high on E. They sound good before they reach the audible stage, but crazy afterward.

Ecstasy doesn't give him that burst of LOVE like it used to. Doesn't make him tell girls how beautiful they are or how he wants to take care of them forever. Now Wolfie mostly feels mean and confused when he takes E. Like when he killed that Jew state trooper who pulled him over. Speeding, reckless driving, carrying concealed—what choice did he really have?

Oba Taylor confessed to that one. Thought taking credit for the murder would wash the mud out of his skin. Oba was a good friend to Wolfie, even if he was mostly Injun. Oba introduced him to his family in the Patch. Didn't object when Wolfie slept with his mostly white sister, Earline.

"Sisters are the best," he tells Linda Sanchez. Half sisters, stepsisters—living in the same house with you like food in the pantry. Always there when the ecstasy takes a hold.

"Earline used to be a pretty girl till crystal meth skanked her out," Wolfie says. "Now her front teeth are gone and her skin looks like the German measles."

Linda Sanchez turns the water off and steps out of the shower. "What the hell you talking about, mister? Why don't you get them pants off and get this over with." She points at her wrist where she would wear a watch—if strippers had any need to keep track of time.

She runs the tip of her tongue over her lips. Hoping to get things moving along more quickly, but all that does is remind Wolfie of what Earline does with her tongue.

"Tardive dyskinesia," he tells Linda Sanchez. He found Earline's diagnosis on the Discovery Channel. On the program where they talk about forty pound tumors and people who wake up from general anesthesia with English accents. Tardive dyskinesia means the tongue has a mind of its own. Crawls and twitches like a leech that's been burned with the hot end of a cigarette.

Tardive dyskinesia is disgusting, and now that Wolfie's got that disgusting tongue picture in his mind he can't get it out even when Linda Sanchez turns sideways so he can see the graceful letter S where her back turns into her ass.

She walks out of the bathroom swishing back and forth like a mime doing a perfect impersonation of a prostitute. It's supposed to get Wolfie interested but his junk shrivels up like it's been soaked in ice water.

She slides her hand down the front of his pants and gropes him the way doctors used to check him for an inguinal hernia back in the day. He turns his head and coughs—automatically—and when he turns back toward the stripper she doesn't look happy.

She keeps her hand in his pants while she kisses him with her mouth wide open. Everything her tongue does reminds Wolfie of tardive dyskinesia.

He asks her, "Want some E?" Figures it couldn't hurt. Put her out of the whoring mood. Make her feel more like girls are supposed to feel when a guy like Wolfie dart tranques them and takes them to a cabin in the Jack Fork mountains for a little Aryan romance.

She clucks her tongue the way his teachers used to do when he got stuck on the first word of a sentence. The way his dad clucks his tongue when Wolfie thinks Jamaicans is a book in the Bible.

She goes down on her knees in front of him. Lets him put a pill on her tongue. Like the Catholics do when they take communion. She unzips his pants, slow and easy, as if she doesn't want to get this thing over quickly anymore. Linda Sanchez is a damn poor excuse for an actress.

"Ain't working." she handles Wolfie like a mentally challenged Four-H member who's just learning to milk a cow.

"Seen it happen before," she tells him.

Problem is, Wolfie's seen it happen before too. Seen it happen a lot lately.

"E blows out the fuses," Linda Sanchez pulls his pants down around his knees. She doesn't resist when he puts his hands on her shoulders.

"Still nothing."

Wolfie's temperature rises a degree with the next five beats of his heart. The higher it goes, the faster his heart beats and the more he understands he's going to have to kill this muddy girl.

"Here it comes," she says. "Your little soldier's standing at attention now."

"Sure is." Now that Wolfie has decided what he has to do. He draws his right hand back and slaps the stripper across the face the way his dad used to slap his mother. It didn't seemed right back then, but now he sees the point.

She crawls away from him backward, rakes her butt across the rough wooden floor of his cabin that hasn't been swept since Wolfie moved in. Heading for the door that Wolfie forgot to lock, way faster than a girl should be able to crab walk.

A whuppin' is what this stripper needs. What Wolfie needs to give her. Dad did that to Wolfie's mother and Wolfie's stepsister. Did it regular to keep them in a respectful frame of mind. Wolfie never understood why—not completely. Not until this moment when his whole body is filled with the need to punish . . . someone, anyone. As long as it's a woman.

"You friggin' e-tard." Linda Sanchez is on her feet again. She walks around him, gathers her clothing off the floor, which she can do pretty easily because his pants are down around his ankles and the room is jumping and spinning like a carousel mounted on a rollercoaster.

He lunges for her. Gets a handful of her hair in his right hand. Swings at her face with his left, but misses.

The stripper crashes her hip into Wolfie's groin. The most painful lap dance ever sends him sprawling on the floor. She screams when he pulls a rope of hair out of her scalp. Keeps screaming as she runs away.

"Doppler effect," Wolfie remembers from another Discovery Channel documentary. His mind is crystal clear now, full of blood and lust.

He refuels with another ecstasy, pulls his pants and underwear off and runs after Linda Sanchez. Something's definitely happening down there now. Something his little soldier thinks is way sexier than filling a muddy girl up with babies.

"Murder!" Wolfie shouts at the trees as he runs by. He hasn't felt this good since he killed that Jew cop and Oba Taylor took the blame.

Mean and powerful and sexy.

6

The person formally known as Wolfie Lafleur. That's how Wolfie thinks of himself as he runs between the trees.

Wolfie Lafleur is the man whose feet hurt like hell as he bloodies them on rocks and broken branches. He's the white supremacist who has a taste for muddy girls. Who is so unlovable his mother left him with a father who hated little boys almost as much as he hated mud people.

Ecstasy temporarily erases Wolfie Lafleur from the universe. The person formerly known as Wolfie wishes it were permanent. Maybe this time it will be. The forest is filled to the brim with ecstasy-amplified moonlight. He can see a hundred yards ahead as he runs between the cedars and post oaks, as he dodges around deadfalls and under broken branches. His reflexes are so fast his mind can't keep up. His lungs fill with air that smells like pine resin. It doesn't contain quite enough oxygen to satisfy, but that's okay. Pain is the glue that keeps his soul attached to his body.

Supernatural glue.

He sees poison ivy vines winding up the trunks of drought-killed trees. Feels three pointed leaves brush against his naked legs as he runs through it. That's one more thing he'll worry about later on when the E wears off and he's a different person.

He doesn't realize he's crying until he tastes the saltwater in his tears. That happens sometimes with ecstasy. God's way of flushing out the soul. Wolfie doesn't like to think about God unless he's had a little ecstasy. Not even when he's listening to a Christian Identity preacher explain how turning the other cheek is meant strictly for the mud races.

Now that Wolfie's ears are tuned to a holy frequency he can hear the voice of God. He knows it's God because the voice sounds just like Charlton Heston in the Ten Commandments movie his father made him watch when it was clear he'd never learn to read the Bible.

He hears something big crashing through the underbrush and remembers Linda Sanchez. She's running toward the Patch—he thinks. His sense of direction is E-radicated at the moment.

The moonlight picks up a bloody tint as it bounces off the tree limbs and the boulders. His spleen hurts from running. His testicles ache, and his brain throbs from being packed too full of things he doesn't want to think about. Like how the only girls he'll ever have are the ones he tranquilizes and rapes.

Except for Oba Taylor's mostly white sister, Earline, who lives in the Patch, where Linda Sanchez is probably headed. The great circle of coincidence brings him to a complete stop.

Wolfie Lafleur is back again. More's the pity. Thoughts of Earline Taylor's missing teeth and overactive tongue blunt the supernatural effects of ecstasy and here he is again. Aware of his nakedness, like Adam in the Garden of Eden after Eve tricked her man into eating the forbidden fruit.

Does he really want to put a baby inside of Linda Sanchez? Does he really want a little bastard with his eyes looking out of a face with high cheekbones and brown skin? Not really. The little soldier between his legs doesn't want it either. What he really wants to do is kill the muddy bitch, slowly and painfully for the crime of . . . it doesn't really matter as long as there is plenty of screaming and lots of blood.

He sees a circle of concentrated light in the forest. Straight ahead, flickering like a poacher's flashlight looking for a deer to freeze in its tracks.

Could be a poacher. Or a hallucination. Or a ghost light.

"Ghost light," Wolfie decides. One of the old Choctaw spirits that live in the Jack Fork Mountains looking to take revenge on a white man. He turns away from the light, and when he turns back he can't see it anymore. Can't remember where it was. Can't remember why he's running through the forest. Whether he's chasing someone or being chased.

The only thing Wolfie knows for sure is that a pill is in his hand. He's been holding onto it ever since this whole thing—whatever this whole thing is—started. His heart rate passed the aerobic stage long ago. His mouth is dry. His sweat glands have gone on strike. He still feels high but he doesn't feel ecstatic anymore. He struggles to focus his eyes on the crescent moon, which is gleaming like the grim reaper's scythe. He tosses the pill into his mouth and feels it plow a furrow in his esophagus all the way to his stomach.

"What will happen now?" Wolfie Lafleur asks the Choctaw spirits who must be in the trees because he can hear them whispering.

He can't make out what they are saying at first, but after a while he can: "Overdose." In English, because the Choctaw never had a word for that.

Wolfie's eyelids are glued together with leftover bad dreams. A hand brushes across his forehead. It pauses long enough to register his body temperature. It's a woman's hand. Cool and soft and full of estrogen. It pulls away—the way they always do—when he tries to grab it.

"Linda?" The name crowds to the front of his thoughts and before he knows it he's telling Linda Sanchez he's sorry for the misunderstanding.

"I was kind of wasted," he says. "Didn't mean to scare you." He hears pine boards squeak as she steps away from him. Loud mouse sounds, amplified by an E-hangover. He pries at his eyes but they remain stuck tight.

Wolfie feels the coarse cloth of a wool blanket covering him. Scraping his lower body, which is still naked. Just the way he left it when his soul broke loose and went on an ecstasy vacation.

The itching from the poison ivy has started. He remembers not caring about that. He remembers Earline Taylor's tongue and missing teeth. And his mother, who's been missing since he was a little boy. And his stepsister, who is in prison now. And Linda Sanchez—the one who got away.

Wolfie has been told that ecstasy molecules have stealthy ways. They hide out in fat cells, safe from detoxification, and when those fat cells are metabolized little bundles of the drug storm out in force, like ninja warriors.

"Flashback," he explains to the girl who might be Linda Sanchez. But he doesn't explain too much because it might not be her at all. It might be a sneaky policewoman trying to trick him out of his right to remain silent.

Thoughts of female trickery make him angry. He can hear the emotion in his voice as he sputters about all the things women have done to him ever since his mother ran away.

"When I was five years old," he tells the woman who has squeaked at least five pine planks away.

His matted eyes give way, because Wolfie is crying.

"It happens like this sometimes." He tries to focus on the girl who's standing all the way across the room from him with her back against a window. The rising sun backlights her with a bloody red halo. The way medieval artists painted the Virgin Mary.

Ninja ecstasy molecules choose that very moment to swarm Wolfie's brain, and he's in love. Red is the color of fertility, and the color of violence, and the color of the floor and walls and everything inside the cabin but the silhouette of the girl with her back to the window. That is blue. The opposite side of the color wheel. The contrast makes Wolfie's world wobble on its axis.

"Linda?" He can't see her face until she takes a step in his direction and looks less like the shadow of a Saint and more like a real live girl.

She says, "Kinta," as she takes another forward step, moving smoothly across the rough wooden planks of the cabin floor as if she's being pulled across a sheet of ice.

"Kinta Minco," she says. "That's my name."

Her eyes go to the white power tattoos on Wolfie's arms. She knows about that kind of thing because she's a muddy girl, like Linda Sanchez. He puts his arms under the scratchy wool blanket. Pretends he's got a chill, even though it's August and the temperature is already in the mid eighties.

Now that his arms are out of sight, Kinta Minco is looking at the way his erection is making the blanket stand up like a circus tent. He tries to force it down, but that only makes it more obvious.

"Where am I?" Wolfie asks.

"My Jack Fork house," is all Kinta Minco tells him, but she says it with a smile that makes his ecstasy flashback more intense.

"Made some tea," she tells him. "Ten-cat mushrooms, moonflower root, and sassafras."

Wolfie doesn't remember getting out of bed, but he is standing, walking toward Kinta Minco with his hands held out the way a five-year-old approaches his mother when he wants to be picked up.

She puts a cup in his hands. It's hot but not hot enough to burn.

"Drink up," she tells him. "It'll chase away all the bad thoughts."

He holds his breath and gulps it down. Bitter liquid, thick as molasses as he gets to the bottom.

"Works fast," she says. "Better sit down until the first wave passes." She pokes him in the chest with her index finger and he falls backward onto the bed. His stomach spasms. His head throbs. His erection wilts like day-old chopped asparagus.

Every depressing thought he has shrinks into a vanishing point at the center of the universe. When they are all gone there is nothing left that's recognizable as Wolfie Lafleur. The world twists into a whirlpool with Kinta Minco at the center. The most beautiful muddy girl ever.

"I'll have to throw you back." She takes him by the hand and leads him toward the door.

"I have things to do and you're much too dangerous to keep around." She walks him to the top of a steep hill and gives him a little push.

"Weebles wobble but they don't fall down." Wolfie says. He turns his walk over to the force of gravity. A higher power. The third step on the Alcoholics Anonymous path to serenity—sort of.

7

Richard doesn't own an alarm clock. It's a matter of Native American pride instilled in him from the time he went to live with Grandma Clementine. He rises with the sun the way Muskogee Creek have done for thousands of years, before wind up watches and electricity and jobs in white men's factories.

Today is different. His internal clock doesn't measure hours and minutes with any accuracy, but he knows immediately it's way past six a.m. His head aches, his mouth tastes like copper pennies and his eyes are full of thick sticky secretions. Richard checks for a body on the floor beside his bed but this is the wrong bedroom and the wrong time.

His knees and vertebrae pop as he climbs out of bed. The skin on his feet feels too thin to keep his bones from popping through. It's a very bad morning and there was no wild time the night before to make up for it. Unless he counts the Tammy-Samantha dream.

Native American holy men are always going on about visions. Does a semi-pornographic dream count as one? It wasn't a burning bush or a pillar of fire, or the spirit of Rainbow Crow with the latest news from the Happy Hunting Ground, but it was pretty intense.

The dream had all the hallmarks of reality, except for floating in the air, and even that felt pretty real. Richard stumbles into the kitchen, and is relieved to see that he's already prepared coffee so all he'll have to do is push a button. He doesn't feel capable of much more.

A breeze that shouldn't be there moves through the room. Insect and bird noises are louder than they ought to be. A gust of wind blows the door all the way open. Didn't he close it before he went to bed? Didn't he lock it?

Richard Harjo stands at the kitchen door. Sees a girl walking toward the woods away from his house. Blue jeans, tailored to fit her with no cloth to spare. A pristine white cotton T-shirt drapes the curvature of her back and breaks over the swell of her hips. Her Long black hair floats in the Oklahoma wind as she turns and smiles at Richard. Her face, her body fit into an empty place in the pleasure center of his brain with a snap that's almost audible.

She waves to him. Backs into the trees and disappears. The kind of magic practiced by deer in hunting season.

Maybe there is a God after all.

Richard sees a sealed envelope on the table covering the popsicle sticks that count the days until Tammy Wynette Biggerstaff's execution. The owl feather he threw away lies on the envelope over two words written in the same loopy Catholic writing as Holabi Minco's.

It says: From Kinta.

It means: Quid pro quo.

The interior of the room where death row inmates spend their last twenty-four hours is identical with all the other H-Unit cells. Solid windowless walls, stainless steel sink and commode. One bunk and one uncomfortable stool are frozen into the cement surface like mammoths trapped in a sheet of ice. Guards call it "The Waiting Room."

Its steel door—painted the same bright yellow color as a Southwestern Bell company truck—is kept locked, even when the cell is empty, except on Moving Day. The cleaning crew sweeps and mops before
and after each occupant. They pray before they cross the threshold.

Richard Harjo sees the yellow Waiting Room door standing open even before he passes through the final security checkpoint. It's ready for Tammy Wynette Biggerstaff when she returns from her last Department of Corrections shower.

Instead of going straight to the cell, Richard follows the sound of running water to the shower room, where the only female death row guard is keeping close watch on Tammy Biggerstaff while pretending to give her privacy.

Madeline, the Choctaw girl who knew Holabi Minco when she was a little girl. Richard is surprised he remembers her name.

Madeline is inside the shower room watching for situations—things that happen when an inmate's time is short. The two male guards wait in the hall so they can run inside if their weak sister calls for help. They trade smirks. They speculate on the appearance of ginger pubic hair.

Richard Harjo moves closer to the guards so they'll be forced to stop. "Have a little respect. The girl dies tomorrow morning."

"Waste of a perfectly fine piece of ass," says one of the men.

"Anton Leemaster." Richard makes a point of reading the name from the guard's Identification tag. Writes it in the air with a pretend pencil. An unspoken threat to make a report but that's something he won't actually do because Anton Leemaster isn't saying anything Richard hasn't already thought.

The guards say, "Sorry, Reverend." As perfectly synchronized as the backup singers for a Motown band.

He stares at them until their noses itch and they have trouble swallowing.

"Jesus is watching you," he tells them. "Others might be watching too." He nods at the open door of the shower. His meaning is clear. The third guard is a woman—one of those sensitive creatures who take offense at everything a man finds natural.

The Reverend Richard Harjo regrets those words immediately, but Richard Harjo, PhD, knows all about group dynamics. Mistrust is the basis for most good behavior. He turns and walks away, leaving the guards to consider whether they've gone too far.

He walks into the Waiting Room, where Tammy Wynette Biggerstaff will live her final day. Oba Taylor will move into the cell she leaves behind. Holabi Minco will take up residence in Oba's cell, and on and on until the twelve cells in the short death row hallway are filled with condemned prisoners. Every H-Unit inmate moves one room closer to the execution chamber. As demoralizing as watching a gallows being built on the prison yard.

Richard sits on the cement bunk where every doomed Oklahoma killer tosses and turns on his last night. Where murderers tell time by counting faces watching them through the viewing window. Every thirty minutes someone checks to make certain the inmate hasn't found a way to cheat the executioner.

Tammy Wynette Biggerstaff says, "I can't believe I got my period," as soon as she walks into the cell.

It's a first for Richard Harjo. The only relevant Bible verse he can remember is Leviticus 15:19-30: . . . if the issue in her flesh be blood she shall be put apart for seven days, and whosoever toucheth her shall be unclean.

It doesn't seem appropriate and he can't think of any psychobabble to fit the present circumstance, so he says, "period." The perfect punctuation for the end of a death sentence.

Tammy sits on her bunk as far from Richard as she can get. "I guess the Medical Examiner will take the tampon out. After . . . you know." She shivers as she says it. Clutches her arms over her breasts the way she did in Richard's vision-dream before she murdered Samantha.

"Anything you need to talk about? Now's the time." The easy inmates want Bible verses. The hard ones confess to crimes no one knows about. What the inmates say is between them and Richard and God and any guards who might be listening outside the door. There's no expectation of privacy in a H-Unit, especially in the Waiting Room.

"What you tell me won't go any further if you speak softly." He rubs his thumb over the gold-paint letters on the cover of the Bible that's been a fixture in this room since 1995. The cover is worn because this Bible has had lots of death row experience. Tammy owns it for a day. Then it will be Oba Taylor's turn then Holabi Minco's. Richard opens it, because that seems like the right thing to do. The pages part at the Book of Revelation—a death row favorite. The final Book of the Bible is where God's true nature shines through. Where he seems like just another psychotic killer.

"Should have been Burdette and Wolfie that I killed," Tammy Wynette Biggerstaff says. "Or maybe one of their friends—men like Oba Taylor. It's men like them who brought this on."

"Killing's never the answer," Richard tells her. Hopes she won't ask him why he'll be walking her into a room where the state of Oklahoma will kill her. Murder and execution. How different are they from a victim's point of view?

"The boys I killed. Two of them looked like Wolfie. The other one looked like Burdette." Tammy says, "Every man looks like Wolfie and Burdette a little."

"Most of them need killin' from time to time." Tammy scoots a little closer. Richard places the Bible between them. She bumps it with her hip, and then pulls back two inches and scratches at the spot touched by the Holy Word.

"When boys get that manly feeling. When a girl knows what's coming' next. When she has her knife. Things naturally fall into place." She switches her gaze between the Bible and Richard, like a wild horse that's seen her first fence and hasn't decided whether to jump or give up her independent ways.

Tammy points to a man's face at the viewing window. "Popsicle man," she says through clenched teeth.

"Anton Leemaster." One of the two guards, whose names Richard has ever bothered learning.

Tammy pushes the Bible into the floor, scoots against Richard Harjo, throws her arms around him. "Don't let them take me yet."

The tumblers click inside the steel door. It opens into the hallway where it's only a few steps to the execution chamber.

"Time to order your last meal." Anton Leemaster stands outside the Waiting Room with a pencil and a clipboard. Madeline looks over his shoulder. The other guards are nowhere to be seen.

"Anything local under fifteen dollars, tax and gratuity included." He poises the pencil over the clipboard as if Tammy Wynette Biggerstaff has been looking at a last-meal menu and should be able to give him her answer now.

"Geraldine's Restaurant is popular," Anton Leemaster tells her. "Their chicken fried is good. Comes with Okra and coleslaw but you can substitute."

Tammy's arms feel like a boa constrictor wrapped around Richard Harjo's chest. He wants to tell Anton Leemaster to leave. Wants to tell him Tammy can't talk about last meals right now. But she's squeezing him so tight, he's afraid he won't be able to fill his lungs again if he wastes his air on words. When he thinks he can't stand it a moment longer, she releases her grip and lets her arms slide down his body. One hand falls into Richard's lap, the other twitches at her side like an insect caught in a spider web.

"Spaghetti-Os," she tells the guard. "Cold, out of the can. I want to eat them with a real metal spoon. Now get the hell out of here and leave me in peace."

Anton Leemaster pokes the end of his tongue between his lips while he prints Spaghetti-Os on his clipboard page. "Have to do some checkin' about the spoon. Might have to go with plastic." He tips his DOC cap and locks the Waiting Room door.

Tammy winces as the bolts slide into place. She puts her arms around Richard Harjo again. Gentle this time. She spreads her fingers so he feels ten points of finger pressure on his back. Her breath floats around his face like a swarm of gnats. Sour with fear and prison food.

8

Tammy pulls back when Richard says, "Tell me how it was when you killed Samantha."

He's taken her by surprise. No one has ever asked Tammy Wynette Biggerstaff about her lesbian lover, much less accused her of Samantha's murder. She doesn't stop him when he unzips her jump suit. Doesn't object when he pulls it over her shoulder where Samantha's name is written in black calligraphy exactly as he saw it when he floated below the ceiling in the murder room.

For the first time in his life, Richard Harjo feels like a real holy man. Somebody on a first name basis with the mystery, even though it's still as mysterious as ever. He sits up taller on Tammy's bunk. If the tattoo is real, so was the murder and if the murder was real, then Richard Harjo had a bona fide vision.

Tammy starts with a feeble denial that quickly turns into a confession. What Richard saw in her bedroom but from a different point of view.

"Sam looked enough like a man to keep the relationship Christian." She's silent for a moment, trying to figure out which part of her sin is worse. She waits for Richard Harjo to call her an abomination. When he doesn't, she scoots close to him again. Throws her arms around him. Tells him she's always been a man's woman. "Except for Sam." Her tears make her words believable. She kisses Richard on the lips.

"There are things we could do, even though I got my period." One of her hands finds its way under his shirt. The other fumbles with his belt.

"Didn't kill her, Rev. Didn't kill nobody but those boys." Tammy grinds her body into Richard Harjo's, uses all the biological powers of persuasion she has at her disposal.

"Sam just disappeared," Tammy tells him. "Just went away is all. Like Burdette and Wolfie did sometimes. She'll be back."

They both turn to the sound of footsteps outside the cell. Samantha's ghost coming for a visit? Anton Leemaster looks through the viewing window and makes a note. Time for Richard to break away from the pretty, doomed girl who is sticky with perspiration and sensuality.

"We can do anything we want, Rev. Jailers won't say nothing." The tip of Tammy's tongue follows the contours of Richard's ear.

"It's OK. Even Jesus must have got that manly feeling now and then." Whiskey voice, the way she talked to Samantha before the knife.

Richard can't push her away, because there's no place on Tammy's body he can touch without participating in her seduction.

"Floating man!" He tells her. His tone and pitch exactly like Samantha's but without the specks of blood.

Tammy freezes into place. Her pupils dilate. The air makes a whistling sound as she fills her lungs. Then she screams loud enough to make Richard's ears ring. Shrill enough to make the viewing window rattle. She rakes her fingernails across his face. Draws four bloody lines as straight and parallel as a popsicle stick calendar.

He tries to hold her off, but every piece of Tammy is quick and sharp and dangerous.

He hears the tumblers click inside the metal door again. Slow deliberate snaps as if the guard on the other end of the key hasn't made up his mind whether to come in.

Anton Leemaster steps into Tammy's cell. Touches her on the neck with a shock stick. One hundred fifty thousand volts and 2.5 milliamps of electricity jump from her to Richard. They thrash and convulse like a pair of spastic lovers and collapse onto the floor.

The guards put Tammy onto her bunk. Position her head so her airway's clear. They drag Richard into the hall.

"What happened, Rev?" The guard named Madeline asks him. "What set her off?"

Richard Harjo can't tell her about Samantha. He won't tell her Tammy is cute and dangerous. So he says, "It must have been Geraldine's Restaurant."

Anton Leemaster checks the pulse in Tammy's neck. He lets his hand drag across her breasts after he's satisfied she's alive and well. "Murderin' girls on death row get pretty antsy, don't they, Rev? Especially when they get their periods."

9

Richard Harjo touches his face as he walks past Oba Leon Taylor's cell. His hand comes away sticky red. The claw marks sting enough to make his eyes water. Oba slouches behind the viewing window. He taps on the glass. Makes a smooching sound loud enough to hear down the entire death row hallway.

He's been moved to Tammy Wynette Biggerstaff's old cell, where he'll stay until it's his turn in the Waiting Room. It's been searched and scrubbed by the custodial team. Scrubbed clean of all the scents and stains of its former occupant with industrial cleaners that would be too toxic in an unventilated room if the occupant had a normal life expectancy.

All the scrubbing in the world can't remove the bad Karma transferred to the cell by every inmate who's been executed in Oklahoma since H-Unit was built. Oba Taylor is next on the DOC death schedule. White supremacist. Member of the Christian Identity Movement. He has no expectation of gubernatorial leniency or Supreme Court intervention.

He murdered a state trooper in Heavener, Oklahoma, "for looking too much like a Jew." Allegedly—as they say on the ten o'clock news.

Oba confessed. Bragged about it to his jury. Threatened the judge with a similar fate during the sentencing phase of his trial. Then he un-confessed after it was too late. Richard Harjo has met lots of killers who un-confessed when they were a few cells away from the Waiting Room.

Oba Taylor has been particularly insistent on his innocence since last Moving Day. "Ain't never killed no one!" He screams at everyone who passes his cell. Everyone—even members of the mud races—who've locked him in H-Unit for "no goddamned reason at all."

If there is such a thing as Hell, Richard figures Oba Taylor has a room reserved. Probably the presidential suite. The inmate made it clear he didn't want "no visit from no goddamned mud preacher." That's what the Christian Identity Movement calls everybody who isn't white. Mud people. Made by God with cheaper materials, after the seventh day when he'd stopped taking pride in his work.

White supremacists take a fundamental view of the violent parts of the Bible but don't believe any verses about tolerance or brotherly love. There's a swastika tattooed over one of Oba's eyes with his pupil in the approximate center. Over the other, he's inked spiraling sevens, which looks a lot like a swastika. Three sevens—arranged like a peace sign with Oba's angry eye at the junction. The number represents 666 + 111. Supersizing the mark of the beast. Richard doesn't know if that makes the movement better or worse than the Antichrist. As far as he can see, there isn't really much difference.

"What you lookin' at, Injun?" Oba's voice carries through H-Unit. The three guards searching Oba's former cell for contraband step into the hallway to watch the show.

Richard doesn't mean to stare at Oba Leon Taylor. The murderer's face is like a billboard advertising hatred. A deep blue number 88 is tatted on his forehead. When he scowls his worry lines make it ripple like a digital advertisement. The eighth letter of the alphabet is H. The number stands for H. H., Heil Hitler. On Oba's chin is the number, 83. That one stands for Heil Christ. It doesn't bother the Christian Identity Movement that Hitler was a suicide and Jesus was a Jew.

It's hard not to stare at a face like Oba Taylor's when it's caged behind reinforced prison glass. The hallway of H-Unit is lit with halogen bulbs, the old fashioned environmentally unfriendly kind that are made in China to light the exteriors of public buildings and the interiors of prisons. The bulbs reflect in a warped line across Oba Taylor's face. Two bright incandescent points of light are superimposed on his eyes, so he looks like a Grade B Movie demon who probably can't be contained in a cell made of steel and cement.

"I ain't did no murder!" If there were bars on Oba's cell, he'd grab them with both hands. He'd rattle them like a wild ape that still remembers the Congo and hates do-gooders like Jane Goodall.

"No friggin' murderer at all." Friggin' is Oba's concession to civility.

"Don't that bother you, Rev? Are you too busy with that sweet little piece of ginger ass next door?" There are no bars to rattle, so Oba pounds on the glass window in the door of his death row cell. Richard knows it will withstand the impact of a bullet without breaking, but he wonders if Oba Taylor is more powerful. Like Superman, only with a swastika on his chest instead of a capital letter S.

"Come closer, Injun. I want to see them scratches that little bitch put on you." The hint of a smile. Three gold teeth. An Alfred E. Newman gap in front, compliments of a prison dentist.

Rumors travel at the speed of light in H-Unit. Every death row inmate knows about the marks on Richard Harjo's face. Like spiraling sevens and swastikas and numbers that compare Hitler to Jesus, the scratches mark Richard as the member of a select group. Men who've been kissed by Tammy Wynette Biggerstaff and survived.

"This cell still smells like her, preacher. Come in and take a whiff." A bigger smile. Oba's breath fogs the viewing window. It turns the ink on his face into smudges, but the hate burns through.

Richard walks closer to the white supremacist's cell. Smiles as if he's not afraid. Wishes he could call on Jesus to protect him, but Jesus is far away and Oba Taylor is very close. And getting closer. Richard wants to stop walking but his legs aren't listening to reason. When he comes to a stop the reflection of his face is superimposed over Oba Taylor's in the viewing window.

The two men are about the same size, but Taylor seems much bigger. The only thing separating them is Richard Harjo's reflection, and a half-inch thick pane of bulletproof glass and the penal code of the state of Oklahoma.

"I knowed Tammy back in the day, Rev. Knowed Burdette Lafleur too, and Wolfie." Richard wanted to call Oba Taylor a liar. Wanted to tell him to let his anger go before they walked him to the death chamber. Wanted to tell him to make peace with the world so he could slip into Heaven without God noticing he's a racist asshole.

"Did you do it, Rev? Did you get into that little murderer's Department of Correction panties?"

Richard watches the fantasy play out in Oba Taylor's eyes. In the coal-black pupils at the exact center of a swastika and spiraling sevens.

"Tell me all about it, Rev." Oba's tongue moves over his lips like he's licking off the final bits of grease left over from a chicken fried steak at Geraldine's Restaurant.

Richard can see Oba Taylor is getting ready for desert. This is how white supremacists bond with Injun preachers. As close as they'll ever come to friendship.

The other thing Richard sees is Oba Taylor's hair. It's not the color or the texture that's usually on a white supremacist's head. African American inmates would call it "Good hair." The kind of hair on Black Seminole heads. Descendants of runaway slaves who lived at the edges of Seminole villages, first in Florida and later in black Oklahoma townships like Bolie and Stella.

Richard Harjo tells the murderer, "Oba is a Creek word. Muskogee language. You know. Seminole speak a version of it too."

"Means bear," Richard tells him. "I remember from bedtime stories Grandma Clementine used to tell me."

"Grandma." The hatred runs out of Oba Leon Taylor's face. His features simplify, like an infant who's fallen asleep in his high chair. His skin looks darker now that the rage is gone. Richard sees Africa in the murderer's face, mixed with Europe, and Native America. Like a lot of people in Oklahoma.

"Bear," Richard says again.

Oba Taylor backs away from the viewing window. Nine feet is as far as his cell will let him go. When he touches the rear wall, he pushes off, screams a combination of a Rebel Yell and a Seminole war cry as he attacks. He crashes his head into the glass and melts to the floor of his cell like a wax figure that's been left in the sun.

"Jesus, Rev." Anton Leemaster stands behind Richard Harjo. Puts a hand on Richard's shoulder. Takes it away and wipes it on his uniform pants. "You shouldn't stir the monkeys up on Moving Day." He bobs his head at Holabi Minco, who is cuffed and shackled, standing between the two other guards in the hallway ready to move into Oba's former cell.

"Hey, Rev." Holabi sounds cheerful. "Got something for you in my pocket." He looks at the chest pocket on his DOC jump suit, left over from the days when the state of Oklahoma allowed H-Unit residents to carry cigarettes.

Three more rungs of the popsicle stick calendar. A name on one of them, mostly hidden inside the pocket. A few looping letters are visible on one of them, as regular as if they came from a printing press.

"I ain't reaching in that pocket," Anton Leemaster says. "You want those sticks, you'll have to take them out yourself."

"Don't suppose you've brought me anything?" Holabi Minco asks.

"The Rev knows that ain't allowed." Anton Leemaster stands away from the inmate. Gives Richard space to go and get his sticks, but Madeline steps in and does it for him.

Her lips move, slowly, easy to read, impossible to hear. "Magic man," as she puts the sticks in Richard's shirt pocket.

"Like I told you, a magic man needs lots of friends. Pleasant dreams, Rev." Holabi winks and walks into his new cell. Next in line after Oba Taylor.

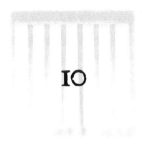

IO

Personal time, comp. time, down time—the Oklahoma DOC doesn't keep track of it for the chaplain who holds hands with death row inmates as they order their last meals and try to figure out whether Hell is any worse than prison.

No one challenges Richard as he passes through the fourteen sets of monitored double doors between him and the employee parking lot. No guards ask to see his ID, because Richard Harjo is now the most recognizable man in H-Unit. The four bright lines across his face tell everybody in the prison everything they need to know. Richard Harjo crossed paths with Tammy Wynette Biggerstaff, who will die with his epithelium under her fingernails because she's already had her last Department of Corrections shower.

Can he ask the medical examiner to clean her nails when he does all the other disgusting things the law requires when someone dies under the most unnatural circumstances ever? Or will Tammy Biggerstaff take part of him to wherever dead murderers go? After they eat their cans of cold Spaghetti-Os and say their last words and Richard tries to convince them of what he's no longer sure of.

"You're going to a better place." Of course that might be true. Anything might be true. Maybe Jesus really made the crippled walk, and raised the dead, and fed the multitudes with loaves of bread and dried fish because Chef Boyardee wasn't around back then.

Richard will spend Tammy's last hour with her, and hope she doesn't attack him again. He'll say God forgives her for murder, and adultery with Samantha, and a lot of things she's probably forgotten at the moment because there's a lot on a girl's mind when the state of Oklahoma plans to kill her and won't put off her execution date because Aunt Flow has come for a monthly visit.

Richard has so much on his mind he doesn't notice the girl walking toward him until his eyes start to follow her. The girl who left a note on his kitchen table and then disappeared into the woods.

Kinta. He thinks of her name in neat looping letters. The way she signed it on the envelope he hasn't given to Holabi Minco.

"Kinta." He says her name quietly, as if he's not sure he has permission. "Haven't delivered your letter."

Richard tries to look away from her but his radar is locked on and he doesn't remember where he left the key.

"Yet," he tells her. "Haven't delivered your letter yet," because even though transporting unauthorized mail to prisoners is a class D felony punishable by up to seven years in the penitentiary he knows he's going to do it.

"Moving Day's too hectic," Richard says. She's close enough so he can feel the heat from her body. Different from the dry summer heat of an Oklahoma August.

He says, "Women's Month," before he can stop himself. Wants to tell her he heard about Women's Month from Holabi Minco, but Richard's voice is on a temporary break. Kinta has captured his attention like a masterwork of art. Like a painting that keeps pulling at his eyes until he understands every detail. She has so many details and they change as fast as Richard Harjo notices them.

"The scratches on my face." He knows she's staring at them. "Not what you probably think."

She reaches out and touches them. Four fingertips follow four clotted bloody trails. Her hand is exactly the same size as Tammy Wynette Biggerstaff's but her touch is gentle. Her eyes are kind and thoughtful. She sniffs her fingertips when she takes them away. Smiles at Richard as if she's learned an amusing secret.

"You look troubled, Rev.," she says. "Holy men are supposed to be at peace. At least they're supposed to look that way."

Richard doesn't feel so holy now. That happened earlier with Tammy, but it didn't last. He wants to tell Kinta all about it but he can't think where he should start.

She puts an envelope in Richard's right hand. "This one's not for Holabi." She closes his fingers over it. Turns and walks away.

Richard wants to follow but his feet won't move.

"Kinta." The word comes out whiskey-hoarse, the way Tammy Wynette Biggerstaff talks when she's about to strike.

Kinta doesn't respond to Richard's voice. She grows smaller with every step away from him. Fifty fluid paces until she vanishes into a point like a lesson in perspective. Gone, but her image is branded in a part of Richard Harjo's mind where he stores things he's not allowed to touch. He looks at the envelope.

To Richard Harjo. From Kinta Minco.

Minco. Richard touches the popsicle sticks in his pocket. *Careful Reverend. My people say this one's got powers.*

He opens the envelope along one edge. Careful not to smudge Kinta's name. The letter inside says:

Dear Rev,

You want to know who Oba Taylor really is, go to the Patch. That's where he started out.

She's sketched a map beneath the letter. His eyes are drawn to a five pointed star over a carefully drawn square with "GRANDMA ANGINA TAYLOR'S HOUSE" printed inside it.

Grandma. The word that calmed Oba Taylor down, if only for a moment. Her house is represented by a large, perfectly proportioned square in the center of a collection of small irregular polygons. THE PATCH is printed over the little community.

THE PATCH, where Oba Taylor started out. Does Richard want to go there? Does he want to find out who Oba Taylor really is?

Yes, if Kinta Minco thinks he should.

II

Richard Harjo knows how dangerous it is to wander off established roads between towns with names like Daisy and Jumbo. Kinta has drawn a marijuana field on his map, and a methamphetamine lab, and an old time moonshine still, all five miles off of Indian Nations Turnpike, hidden by rolling hills that only Oklahomans would give a name as colorful as the Jack Fork Mountains.

"STAY AWAY FROM THIS." Is written in large looping Kinta Minco letters over every danger zone on the map. A broken line represents the road. Cartoon boulders and trees are strategically placed for the maximum esthetic effect. The kind of map Pooh Bear and Christopher Robin followed through the Hundred Acre Wood.

The trail ends at GRANDMA ANGINA TAYLOR'S HOUSE. Grandma's first name is a medical condition—a pain in the chest treated with tiny tablets of nitroglycerine.

Richard's grandmother used nitroglycerine tablets. Dissolved them under her tongue when she thought about her son too much. "They don't fix a broken heart, but they make it ache less," she told him.

"This kind of nitroglycerine don't explode, but sometimes it makes your head feel like it's going to." She'd go off into a dark room and wait out the pain. "Dark is good for the headache but it makes the heartaches worse."

Richard's head throbs a little when he finds the hidden road to Grandma Angina Taylor's house on the far side of a dried up streambed behind a rest stop on Indian Nations Turnpike. It's marked by a pair of X's scratched into sandstone boulders. Two illiterate signatures of the secret road crew that laid out a path people like Richard aren't supposed to know about.

He drives past tall fuzzy green plants that look like botanical immigrants from Mexico. There are keep out signs drawn in cruel red letters that remind him of the bloody marks across his face.

What will Grandma Angina Taylor think of Tammy Biggerstaff's claw marks? There probably isn't much that would shock a woman with a grandson like Oba Leon Taylor.

The odor of ammonia penetrates his windows as he drives past a pair of ruts that—according to Kinta's map—lead to a meth lab and certain death. He holds his breath until he can't hold it any longer, and then he's reached his destination.

The Patch, a starting point for people like Oba Taylor, an ending point for people like Richard Harjo.

Grandma Taylor's house sprawls across the clearing. Newer sections have been added while the older ones are left to rot. The original dwelling segment is four termite-infested log walls built at the edge of the woods. Its roof collapsed so long ago trees grow inside. The log house connects to a newer unpainted wood frame structure with weathered boards nailed across the doors and windows. That merges into a modern rectangular prefab construction with hail-damaged aluminum siding. The only thing the building styles have in common is an ugly esthetic. Old ugliness merging into new. Future ugliness still in the planning stages.

Richard steps out of his car, counts five small, dilapidated mobile homes spaced out around the central building like moons orbiting a dying planet.

If you want to know who Oba Taylor really is, go here.

Richard thinks now might be an excellent time to get back in touch with his religion but is afraid Jesus would see through his change of heart.

"Hold it there, partner." The voice comes from behind Richard Harjo. Not angry. No overt threats, but when a man pays an unexpected call to Ms. Angina Taylor he has to be careful.

Richard raises his hands slowly. Holds them out at a wide angle, as if he's the letter Y in a Village People YMCA video. He turns slowly toward the voice that sounds like it belongs to a man with a gun, and sure enough it does.

A shotgun. Too old for Richard to recognize the brand. Two barrels with a hammer for each one. The gunman pulls them back one at a time.

"What you doin' here?" A cowboy hat, naturally, and a pair of cowboy boots that look well past their second resoling job. The gunman's skin is too dark for a Native American and too light for an African. He limps as he takes a step toward Richard Harjo and raises the shotgun half way to his shoulder.

Richard smiles at him like he really wouldn't mind dying on the spot.

"Friend of Oba's." First lie he's told since he left the prison. "Heard he used to live here." The marks across his face itch so much he has to lower one of his hands long enough to scratch them.

"Here to pay respects?" the gunman says.

Richard nods. Everything he says from this point forward is going to be a lie so he decides to practice his Indian ways. The hinges on Grandma Taylor's front door squeak. Footsteps behind Richard move across the litter-strewn yard. A hunting dog sniffs at his crotch and growls.

"Friend of Oba's" the gunman tells the person behind Richard.

"Oba don't have many friends." Woman's voice, full of doubt and phlegm. "Where you know him from?"

"Prison." He leaves the word hanging in the air. Gives Oba's people a few seconds to draw conclusions.

"Done time with him before he went to H-Unit." Richard's bad grammar sounds fake, but it's good enough for the gunman. He lowers one of the shotgun hammers.

Half way there.

The woman steps in front of Richard. Mid-forties? It's hard to tell. Her white skin has been marked by methamphetamine acne and tortured by the sun. Her greasy blonde hair is braided into a dozen or so mismatched pigtails. Going for a scary Medusa look.

She touches the marks on his face. Sniffs at her fingertips the way Kinta did. Takes a smile far enough for Richard to see she has no front teeth.

"Too much Indian blood to hang with Oba's skinhead friends. You a rapist?" The tip of her tongue pokes through the place her incisors used to be. Far enough to cast a shadow on her chin.

Six more weeks of winter, is what Richard Harjo thinks. "Old time burglar," is what he says. Richard hasn't planned any of these lies so his voice travels uphill at the end of the sentence.

The gunman takes his finger out of the trigger guard. "Oba was always Miss Angina's favorite. Probably still is—even though she's passed. Any friend of his . . . ."

Richard lowers his arms. The dog picks a hand, sniffs it, licks it, and trots away.

"My name's Earline," the woman tells him. "Oba's white sister." The word white comes out with a smile that doesn't try to hide her missing teeth.

"Man with the shotgun's name is Otto." The cowboy lowers the other hammer on his shotgun, and pinches the brim of his cowboy hat between his thumb and trigger finger.

"Oba's colored brother," Earline says. "I'm tellin' you that so you know who'll kill you if you steal something from inside." Her words are thick and wet. Richard looks at grandma's house so he won't have to watch her tongue explore her Caucasian cheeks.

"People call me Richard. Wouldn't steal nothing from Oba's people." The double negative sticks in his throat enough to give him a slight stutter. He walks in front of Oba's colored brother and his white sister but their shadows loom ahead of him. The limping shadow in a cowboy hat and the lurching shadow with the Medusa hair, like a pair of monsters from the spirit world that Richard is starting to believe might be real after all.

"Got to keep the screen door closed." She pushes him aside. Richard Harjo hasn't gained enough trust to touch the door.

"Too many flies have already got in." Earline's tongue crawls over her upper lip, all the way to the tip of her nose, then retracts like a mechanical ruler.

She didn't exaggerate about the flies. Exaggeration might be impossible in Oba-Taylor-Land. Grandma is laid out on a makeshift wooden table in front of a settee. Richard had forgotten all about that word until this moment. It's perfect for Grandma Taylor's living room.

Mourners pace around the body drinking Moonshine whisky from Burger King glasses, smoking cigarettes. One of them blows a stream of smoke over Grandma's face.

"Keeps the flies from layin' eggs," someone tells him. It doesn't matter who. The people in this room are interchangeable. Not identical, but different in shocking ways that make them impossible to differentiate. Twisted postures, freakishly long or short limbs, crossed eyes, walleyes, eyes that move in separate orbits. Clubfeet, bare feet, missing feet. Hair styled by the Marquis de Sade. Grandma's mourners are as different and indistinguishable as sideshow freaks.

Everybody wears some kind of holstered pistol. Old time cowboy six shooters are the favorite. Most of them have fancy hand tooled gun belts adorned with turquoise beads and silver squash blossoms. The men and some of the women fasten their belts with buckles that look like they might have been awarded by the World Wide Wrestling Federation. Names have been pressed into the leather. Country names with halogen endings—Ludine, Earline, Evangeline—are most common for the women. The men favor Germanic names: Siegfried, Aksel, and Otto.

The room smells of gun oil, corn whiskey, and early stage decomposition. Richard guesses Grandma has been dead at least three days. Bloating has given her a body type very much like Oba's. Her hair is like his too. Straight, but not limp. It's been washed, dusted in cornmeal, combed, and decorated with a pair of antique clips that look like they might have been made from real tortoise shells. Her skin is the color of a medium rare steak. All things considered, she's the most normal looking person in the room.

Lividity makes it impossible to identify Grandma Angina's race precisely. Richard suspects it would be equally impossible if she were alive, but she's definitely one of Oba Taylor's mud people.

"What's that in your pocket?" Earline pokes him in the ribs. He turns and looks at her. Wishes he hadn't. Her tongue pokes through her lips and draws a slime-trail speckled with tobacco flakes across her chin.

He has no idea what she's talking about until her hand touches the popsicle sticks in his shirt pocket.

She pulls the first one out. "Got a name on it."

"L-o-r-a-d-o M-e-n-d-e-z." She sounds it out. Her tongue moves through extra-oral calisthenics that have no relationship to the words.

"Lorado Mendez." She says it quickly this time. Touches the popsicle stick to her hyperactive tongue. "Wrote in blood."

No one in the room doubts this woman can recognize the taste.

"Why is that Mister Richard?"

"Well, Holabi . . . ." Every eye is on Richard as he tries to think of a diplomatic way to tell this crowd about Holabi Minco's stick calendar and how Oba Taylor's name should be written on that stick because he's the next to die.

"Maybe on these other sticks." As he pulls the remaining sticks out of his pocket, Richard Harjo realizes what might happen if one of them has Oba Taylor's name on it.

"Blank." Nothing but a little orange stain left over from the sticks' pre-calendar days, and something else, stuck to one of them.

"Owl feather," Richard tells the crowd. A breeze gusts through the screen door and catches the feather, breaks it free of the sticky residue, carries it to the ceiling, around collections of spider webs, under water stains. The mourners watch silently, like spectators at a public hanging.

The feather falls like a maple seed, turns in circles and lands on Grandma Angina's lips.

"Witch!" Earline shrieks and tries to open the wounds Tammy Biggerstaff gave Richard earlier today. He pushes her aside, but falls over Grandma. Sees people reaching for their pistols as Miss Angina's bloat collapses with a flatulent noise, and the table crashes to the ground.

A dozen pistols are drawn by the time he gets to his feet, so he reaches for the only shield available. Richard Harjo lifts Grandma by her hair. Holds her in front of him like a mannequin salesmen exhibiting his wares. The mourners back into each other. Try to put space between themselves and the witch who's dancing backward out the door with grandma's body like a zombie version of Fred Astaire and Ginger Rogers.

All except Earline. She crashes a shoulder into Grandma. Rigor mortis has loosened its grip, so Grandma flops on top of Earline when her hair tears loose in Richard's hands.

He makes it all the way to his car before the shooting starts. Looks in his side view mirror, counts three muzzle flashes in the doorway. Sees a young man with a shaved head step around the side of Grandma's house holding a modern semi-automatic pistol in a shooter's stance. Hears Earline shout, "Get him Wolfie," as she pushes her way through the crowd congesting the doorway.

Earline shouts, "Kill the bastard, Wolfie," followed by a series of words that sound profane but Richard can't be sure because he's never heard them before. He slumps in the driver's seat to make a smaller target and grinds his engine to a start.

The warning etched in glass across the bottom of the mirror says, "Objects may be closer than they appear." An Omen. One more thing Richard Harjo is starting to believe in. A pair of bullets shatters his rear window and exit through his windshield, but no one follows as he drives past the marijuana fields and the bootlegging operation, and the meth lab. He doesn't slow down as he bounces across the dry streambed and drives back onto Indian Nations Turnpike.

"Now I know who Oba Taylor really is." He looks at the two swatches of Grandma's hair on the front seat of his car and the pair of antique tortoise shell clips. He knows a little more about himself too. He picks up one of the clips.

He's lied to Oba Taylor's white sister and colored brother. He's stolen from the dead. Mutilated a body—at least that's not one of the commandments.

"Dear God." Richard composes a prayer in his mind, but doesn't get past the salutation. He starts to say, Amen, but doesn't. It's probably too late to do any good.

"Mister?" A woman's voice from the floorboards between the front seat and the back. Richard can't see her in the rear view mirror until she raises herself onto the bench seat.

She gets a look at the claw marks on his face and asks the obvious question: "You a rapist?"

"Preacher." He thinks maybe he should tell her about his PhD in psychology, but this is probably not the time to flesh out his resume.

"I think I might have herpes if that makes any difference." She's a pretty girl with hard Native American eyes and soft bronze skin blemished with a couple of facial bruises that look fairly new.

"You were talking to yourself." She says. "Thought I should interrupt before you said something you didn't want me to hear."

Richard feels a front tire crunch gravel as it drifts onto the shoulder beside the highway. He jerks the wheel, fights a skid into submission.

"You sure you're not a rapist?"

"Positive."

"Well then, I guess I don't really have herpes." She waits a couple of seconds and then asks if Richard can drop her off at Nasty's Titty Bar. As if that's a place every man in Oklahoma will know.

"Name's Linda Sanchez." She extends her hand over the front seat, wiggles her fingers until Richard touches them with his.

"Richard Harjo. Pleased to meet you."

They look at each other in the rearview mirror until he drifts off the road again. "Fasten your seatbelt," he tells her as they approach the Daisy exit. "And tell me which way to go."

12

Anton Leemaster is smoking in the parking lot at 5:30 in the morning as Reverend Richard Harjo pulls into his assigned parking space.

"Taking a little break." He blows a smoke ring. Richard watches it rise into the air and disappear.

"Might know that one would show up on an execution day." Leemaster points his cigarette at the trees growing at the edge of the parking lot.

Richard expects a collection of protestors, but they usually gather at the front of the prison with the TV camera crews. "I don't see anything." He checks his watch. It's synchronized with the clock in the death chamber.

"Five thirty-two," he says. "Tammy Wynette Biggerstaff dies in exactly thirty minutes." He should have been here earlier but he wrestled with nightmares last night—starring Grandma Clementine and Grandma Taylor—and slept through his alarm.

"Almost too late." He watches the second hand brush number twelve and start the next minute of Tammy Biggerstaff's countdown.

"It's already too late for Tammy," Anton Leemaster says. "Don't really matter if she says a prayer at the last minute. Does it, Rev.?"

Richard Harjo follows the guard's gaze and sees a figure move between two trees. Invisible until she steps out of the forest, but now impossible not to see.

"Holabi's daughter." The guard spits on the tarmac. Tosses his cigarette on the ground. Crushes it with his heel. "Came to see her old man regular for a while, back when I worked visitation. Spoke Choctaw through the visit-phones so I couldn't eavesdrop."

Kinta Minco walks a few steps into the parking lot. She waves. Holds her hand in the air until Richard waves back.

"She watched my reflection in the glass while she talked to her daddy," Anton Leemaster says. "Used to smile at me, like she was interested. Used to hang around and talk." The guard lights another cigarette.

"All at once she just quit coming." He blows another smoke ring. The perfect circle hovers between him and Richard until a gust of wind blows it away.

"Address she put in the visitors log was made up." Leemaster tries for another smoke ring, but this one loses its shape. "Checked it out, Rev." He flips his cigarette onto the tarmac surface of the parking lot beside the Pittsburgh County Medical Examiner's van that will haul Tammy Biggerstaff's body to the morgue. The cigarette explodes in a shower of sparks.

"No real address. No Social. No birth certificate registered anywhere. She don't exist on paper. The way she disappears, maybe she don't exist at all." He takes a step toward Kinta. She vanishes into the trees.

"Poof. She's gone," Leemaster says. "Witchy little girl."

"You know a lot about Holabi's daughter," Richard says.

"More than you think, Rev." Anton Leemaster drops his voice to a low rumble. The way a man tells dirty jokes to another man when women might overhear. "She'd watch me through those sexy Injun eyes. Like there was gonna be something between us, you know?"

The guard checks the time again. "Better go, Rev. Or you'll miss holdin' hands with Tammy one last time." Anton Leemaster tries to laugh, but all he can manage is a snort. "I'll warm up my shock stick in case she wants to scratch you up some more."

Tammy Wynette Biggerstaff rocks back and forth on the edge of her bunk and mumbles words Richard Harjo can't understand. He doesn't interrupt her because they might be a prayer. The door to her cell is open—a suicide watch disguised as trust. A pair of guards stand outside ready to rush in if Tammy turns violent. Minutes move slowly but relentlessly, the way they always do in the last half hour when every second has the condemned inmate's full attention. She reaches for Richard's wrist. Turns it so she's face to face with his Timex. She holds her breath while the second hand completes a circuit.

"They say time passes slow when you're watching it. That ain't the least bit true." She inspects the ruins of her fingernails.

"Chewed to the quick. Guess I swallowed the part of you I scratched off your face." Tears roll down Tammy Biggerstaff's cheeks, following tracks left by the tears she cried earlier today. "Sorry I did that, Rev."

A murderer apologizing for a scratch.

"It's okay," Richard tells her. He wants to tell her everything will be okay. He wants to tell her God won't hold anything against her, and there really is a better place she's going to in ten more minutes. He can't stop himself from looking at his watch.

"They don't put a clock in the Waiting Room." Tammy tells him. "So you can't see how long you've got left before they . . . come for you." She looks at the two guards standing in the hall. "They won't have to come too far, will they, Rev?"

It's quiet in this part of H-Unit. Not like in general population where steel doors slam and men scream obscenities at the world twenty-four hours a day. It's especially quiet on execution day.

A guard in the hallway clears his throat. Richard watches Anton Leemaster walk past carrying his red and white cooler of popsicles. He stops at the door. Looks at the cooler, then at Richard.

"Popsicle, Rev? It's hot as Hell in the chamber." He smiles at the word Hell, where Tammy Biggerstaff will be going in less than ten minutes.

"How 'bout you, Tammy? Want to cool down now so it'll take less time to reach room temperature?"

"Get out of here, Leemaster." Richard's tone is angry, but without a hint of violence. Too much violence is already scheduled to take place in—he checks his watch—eight minutes. "Have a little decency."

Tammy looks at the open door like she might make a break for it. Richard puts an arm around her shoulders. Feels her muscles tense and then relax. Feels waves of panic radiate from her body.

"Not worth it," he tells her. Anton Leemaster smiles and moves toward the execution chamber. Four steps between the execution room and Tammy's cell. Inmates call it the final mile. Named for an old movie from the thirties. Nobody has seen that film for three quarters of a century but the name stuck.

Richard knows the guards won't leave the door open when Oba Taylor's moment comes. Tammy is a special case. She killed more people than Oba. Did it with more violence, but she is a woman—a petit, good-looking woman—and nobody, not even Madeline, will admit to being afraid of her.

"You're part of this, Rev." She watches the three hooded executioners move past the open door. Their identities will be kept secret from everyone except the warden and DOC death row personnel. And payroll, of course. Each one will receive a hundred dollar bill when the job is finished.

"You're the best part of a real bad thing. I know you don't want to be, but you are."

Something clunks against the wall between the Waiting Room and the execution chamber.

"Come into my chamber said the spider to the fly." Tammy walks over to her stainless steel toilet, kneels before it and throws up her Spaghetti-O's.

A new kind of graven image. Richard Harjo wonders if God had this in mind when he fleshed out the second commandment.

The metaphor isn't lost on Tammy. "I'm on my knees, Rev. Shouldn't I be talkin' to Jesus? Shouldn't I be doin' something?"

"If there's anything you need to tell me, Tammy. Now's the time." He stands beside Tammy Biggerstaff as she throws up again. Puts his hand on her shoulder. Feels her muscles contract under the gentle pressure of his fingers. Richard Harjo's touch is not a comfort to Tammy. No man's touch has ever been.

She looks up at him like she's about to make a full confession. Like she's finally ready to tell him about Samantha's murder. "But what if the Governor calls, Rev? What if the Governor decides those boys was bad enough to kill after all. Samantha will be another charge."

Anton Leemaster clears his throat. "It's time to go, Tammy. We won't put you in shackles if you promise not to pitch a fit."

"Let me brush my teeth?" She stands. Walks over to her sink. Starts to reach for her toothbrush but Anton Leemaster pulls her away.

"Don't worry about your breath, Tammy. Nobody's gonna kiss you goodbye."

Richard Harjo still hasn't decided whether people have souls that pass through to the other side, but he knows there is such a thing as cruelty. He should say something to the guard. He should stand up for Tammy Wynette Biggerstaff who has only a few minutes to live, but instead he says, "Come on, Tammy. I'll hold your hand."

He's part of this, like Tammy said, whether he wants to be or not. Richard will walk Tammy Biggerstaff to her death the way holy men have done with human sacrifices for thousands of years. Talk to her about higher purpose, and everlasting life in paradise only four feet from the Waiting Room. Instead of tossing Tammy into a volcano, he'll watch them strap her onto a table that looks like a stainless steel cross. He'll watch them put a needle into her arm, fill her veins with drugs meant to be used by doctors who swore to "do no harm."

"Maybe it won't be so bad," he lies.

He's seen it done many times before. It's quiet. It's dignified after a fashion. But it's always bad.

13

"Will Wolfie and Burdette be here?" Tammy looks at the curtained window where the interested parties will watch her execution.

"No," Richard tells her. "Not on the witness list." Holds eye contact so she'll believe he checked. He's lied to Oba Taylor's family, stolen from the dead. Now he's comforting a dying woman with a promise that's probably another lie.

Madeline, and a guard whose name Richard doesn't remember, and a technician in green scrubs strap Tammy Biggerstaff down. Richard holds her hand while the tech unzips her jumpsuit and presses adhesive pads to her chest. The pads are attached to copper leads that transmit her heartbeat over phone lines to the State Medical Examiner's office in Oklahoma City.

The tech wears a telephone headset so he can take directions from the ME.

"Yes sir," he moves one of the adhesive pads. Adjusts the leads. "She's a little tachycardic," he tells Richard and the guards. "ME says that's normal under the circumstances."

"Means your heart's beating a little too fast," he says to Tammy. "Nothing to worry about." Reassuring tone. Reassuring smile. Richard wonders how long he'll last on this job.

The three hooded executioners peek out from their private room where each of them will push a button and no one will know exactly which one starts the process. They duck back inside when the tech gives them the thumbs up sign. The Emperor of Rome gave the very same sign when he decided a gladiator would be spared. Here it means the opposite.

Curtains snap open so the witnesses can see what happens in the final minutes. Tammy is lying flat on the execution table so she can only see the ceiling of the witness room.

"No Wolfie. No Burdette." Richard reassures her. He sees the sheriff of Pittsburgh County, a female reporter from *Tulsa World*, the assistant warden, and Anton Leemaster with his box of popsicles. There are three women Richard doesn't recognize. Tear-streaked, grim faces identify them as the mothers of the three boys Tammy killed. Two men, one in his late fifties, the other in his thirties, are separated from the women by an empty chair. Their heads are shaved to stubble like the man who shot at Richard back at Grandma Taylor's place. The man Earline called Wolfie. Richard remembers the gunman's pistol and his baldhead but can't be sure of the face.

The two men might be relatives of the victims, but Richard is pretty sure they are Wolfie and Burdette Lafleur.

He squeezes Tammy's hand a little harder and reinforces his harmless lie. "They're not here Tammy. Even the DOC wouldn't be that cruel."

The technician says, "Big stick," and hits a vein first time. Says, "Sorry, Miss, but if I didn't do it somebody else would."

Tears run into Tammy's ears as she looks from the technician to Reverend Richard Harjo.

He wants to repeat what the technician said. Tell her it's not his fault this is happening. Anton Leemaster waves from the witness room. He smiles and passes popsicles to the observers because it's still August and the air conditioning still can't keep up.

It's hot inside the chamber too but Tammy is trembling. Her hand squeezes Richard Harjo's hard enough to make him squirm.

The warden enters the execution chamber. Doesn't look at anyone as he walks to his position beside the observers' window where the interested parties can't see him. He keeps his eyes trained on a telephone mounted on the wall. Asks Tammy if she has anything to say. She had the opportunity to write her last words down. To let the warden read them aloud—the only way to make sure the newspapers got it right—but Tammy didn't want to put anything in writing, in case the Governor was having second thoughts.

"Want to whisper to the Rev."

She still thinks the telephone on the wall might ring, so Richard knows it's not a true confession. He leans over. Hears words run out of her like a slow leak in a tire. The air coming out of Tammy smells like vomit, and Spaghetti-O's, and panic.

Richard holds his breath. Only a minute more. He should be able to hold his breath that long but he uses all his oxygen in the first few seconds. The world spins and turns dark around the edges, but the thought of inhaling Tammy's final words is enough to keep him from breathing.

Her whispers sound like a crowd chanting simultaneously. Louder and louder, until they suddenly stop. Richard slumps forward. Steadies himself on Tammy's gurney. A flash of light explodes inside his head. It concentrates into a single dot a million miles away. Grows larger as he and Tammy Wynette Biggerstaff fly toward it. Through a tunnel as dark as the inside of a coffin.

Like near death experiences he's read about. This is as near to death as anyone can come and still return. The light at the end of the tunnel is the color of the moon. Bats fly through it. Owls fly across it. Human figures wait on the other side.

"One of them is Samantha," Tammy says. "She wants me to tell you." The air inside the tunnel is too thin to carry her voice, but Tammy's words are clear as she describes exactly where Samantha's body is hidden.

"Nothing but bones by now," she says. "Sleeping underneath the house where I killed her. Burdette and Wolfie's place." As she tells him the address a map draws itself in his mind. It looks like the one Kinta Holabi gave him.

Air rushes into Richard's lungs. Clears his head enough so he doesn't collapse on top of Tammy Biggerstaff.

Someone is talking to him but his mind barely has enough oxygen to process the words. "Strangest final statement I've ever heard."

The warden—Richard finally recognizes the voice. His mind wobbles like a top that's running out of spin. A few more deep breaths and he remembers where he is. What he's doing here. He looks at Tammy Biggerstaff. Her dead eyes are open. So is her mouth. Spaghetti-Os are stuck between her teeth. She doesn't look like she's asleep.

"Never heard any last words like that," the Warden says. "And I've heard a lot."

Richard pictures Samantha's final resting place in his mind. Wonders if everybody in the death chamber heard what Tammy told him.

"Floating man!" the warden says. "You ever hear any last words like that?"

"Once before," Richard tells him. "Only once before."

Tammy Biggerstaff's hand still has ahold of Richard Harjo's. He pulls her fingers back one at a time as if he's peeling a banana. As he lifts his hand away, Tammy's fingers close again—nothing left to hold her in the land of the living.

"Floating man," The Warden says. "What do you suppose she meant by that?"

Richard could tell the Warden, "I'm the floating man," but that would lead to a lot of questions he doesn't want to answer, so he watches the guards and the technician unhook Tammy from the wires and the plastic tubing. They unstrap her from the gurney and slide her into a plastic bag.

"Last ride." The technician looks at the witness room. Explains what's happening like he's the MC of a game show. "She'll go to Pittsburgh County Morgue for an autopsy. Not that there's any doubt about the cause of death."

14

Holabi Minco asks, "Who's visiting me today?" as soon as Richard steps into his cell. "The Reverend Richard Harjo? Psychologist Richard Harjo? Somebody in between?"

Titles don't seem to matter much inside Minco's cell—or anywhere in H-Unit. "I held her hand while she died," Richard says. "Stayed with her until she . . . ."

"Passed over." Minco finishes the thought. "They call it that for a reason."

"It seemed real." Richard looks at the hand that held Tammy Biggerstaff's while her spirit slid toward the light at the end of the tunnel. He wiggles his fingers, amazed they are still under his control.

"Still seems real." Richard shakes his Tammy-hand, as if he can throw the feeling off.

Minco says, "You've come to a fork in the road, Rev. Sooner or later you've got to choose a path."

Richard clenches and relaxes his fingers as if the feel of death were a cramp he could work out, given enough time. "There's an explanation for this."

"A scientific explanation." Already trying to redefine the magic. Already converting mysticism to chemistry and biology. He tells Minco about the pineal body buried in the center of the brain that secretes hallucinogenic chemicals when the central nervous system is starved for oxygen. "Those chemicals explained everything—until I saw . . . ."

"A dead girl's bones, lying underneath a house," Richard says. "At an address in the real world." Something tangible. Something he can check out—if he has the courage.

He tells Minco the bones have a name. "Samantha."

"They don't want to be there anymore," he says.

The idea is not foreign to Holabi Minco. "Souls come in two pieces. That's what the old time Choctaw say."

He holds up two fingers like a victory sign. "The shalup, goes to the happy place. The shilombish stays with the bones."

Richard thinks of Samantha's haunted bones lying in a crawl space underneath Burdette and Wolfie Lafleur's empty house.

"The house is abandoned," he tells Minco. Something Tammy Biggerstaff couldn't know unless Samantha told her. Something Samantha would know because she still has a connection to her bones.

"Shilombish." Richard says. Giving Samantha's ghost a name makes it seem more tangible.

"You didn't come here to talk about spirits." Holabi Minco holds out his hand to remind Richard of the purpose of his visit.

"The envelope." Richard lifts Kinta's envelope out of his back pocket with the hand that held Tammy Biggerstaff's while her spirit crossed over. He still has time to change his mind about committing a class D felony. He can still walk out of the cell and leave Holabi Minco to his own devices. Leave him to his popsicle sticks with the names of condemned inmates written on them in his blood. Leave him with the owl feathers smuggled to him by a guard who fell under his spell when she was a little girl.

Richard puts the envelope in Holabi's open hand. Releases it like a well -trained hunting dog bringing a bird to his master.

"Broke the law for me," Holabi Minco says. "not a big law but it's a step." He holds the envelope to the light. Inspects the glue line on the flap.

"Ain't been opened." Minco doesn't open it either. He tosses the envelope into the plastic trashcan beside his stainless steel toilet. "No need to look inside Rev. You brought it. That's all I need to know."

"The guards will find it when they go through the trash." Richard says. "Anton Leemaster . . . ."

"It's his job, ain't it Rev.? He takes it serious, don't he?"

Richard walks over to the window in Holabi's cell door. The female guard, Madeline, is standing on the other side.

"She won't tell on you Rev. Choctaw girls don't carry tales—except to other Choctaw girls."

Like Kinta.

Holabi smiles at Richard like he can read his mind. "You and my girl got something in common, Rev." He crosses his arms and says nothing more until Richard shows some interest. A raised eyebrow is enough.

"Look at the name scratched beside the door, Rev. It's old and the scratches ain't deep but you can still read it."

There are a dozen shaky names scratched into the hard, gunite surface. The third one down is, Richard Harjo.

"You and my girl both have murderers for daddies."

Richard runs the tip of his finger over the scratches. Feels a connection he hasn't felt since he was ten years old. When he talked to his father through a prison visitation phone. Their hands were separated by a half-inch-thick, wire-reinforced, safety-glass barrier, but he could feel emotion soaking through from the other side.

"Sorry I killed your mom, Richie. Sorry it turned out so bad."

Grandma Clementine took him away after that. They prayed together. Prayed for his father to find peace before he passed over.

"It was bad for him at the end." Richard doesn't mean to talk about his father, but it spills out of him like Tammy Biggerstaff's Spaghetti-Os.

"I didn't see it, but Grandma Clementine told me."

"Nobody forgave him. Nobody helped him to the other side. There ought to be someone helping you at the end, no matter what you did."

"So you became a holy man." Minco waits for Richard to answer, but he's said everything he has to say.

"Before you had any idea what it means to be part of this." Minco stands beside Richard, puts an arm around his shoulders, walks him to his bunk where the stick calendar is laid out.

"You already took Lorado's sticks. Ready for the next in line?" He places the next group of sticks into Richard's pocket.

"Heavy," Richard tells him. "Heavier than Tammy's or Lorado's."

"A psychologist couldn't feel the difference, but a holy man can tell." Holabi says, "Don't forget what you brought back from Grandma Angina's house."

Richard hasn't mentioned the visit to Holabi, but Kinta knows. Maybe she told Madeline. Does Minco mean the tortoise shell hair clips or Linda Sanchez?

"Wouldn't be a quest unless you brought something back," Holabi tells him. "Whatever you have rightly belongs to Oba."

The clips. Richard's short experience with Linda Sanchez convinced him she'd never really belong to any man.

The mechanical lock on Holabi Minco's cell door rattles as the tumblers fall into place. Anton Leemaster steps into the entryway. He doesn't make the inmate stand against the wall but he holds his truncheon in the ready position. Smacks it against his palm as a show of strength, as if watching Tammy Biggerstaff die had given him power.

Richard faces Leemaster, watches the cruel smile on the guard's face flatten. Knows without turning around that Holabi is the one smiling now, because he's the stronger of the two even though he is the one in the DOC jumpsuit waiting his turn in the death chamber.

"Wait here for a minute Rev," Anton says. "The Hooded Men are coming back now that Tammy's done. I want the witch to see them."

The executioners. There's no back way out of H-Unit. Cell doors stay closed while the witnesses leave, but Anton Leemaster wants Holabi Minco to see the men who'll push the buttons when his time comes. The men who will turn him into meat, and bones, and bitter memories.

Richard wonders if half of Holabi's Choctaw soul will remain with those bones?

Three pairs of synchronized footsteps move four paces down the hall. They stop in front of the Waiting Room. Like butchers window-shopping at a slaughterhouse.

Richard hears them stumble when Oba Taylor crashes into his cell door.

"He can't get out," Leemaster tells them. "That one's locked up tight." He smiles at the executioners, brave behind their masks when their victim is a little girl strapped to a stainless steel gurney.

The Hooded Men look into Holabi Minco's cell as they pass by. The inmate has moved closer to the door while Leemaster watched the action in the hallway.

Richard sees the fear in their eyes through the holes in the executioner's hoods. Nervous eyes doubtful of the strength of Oba Taylor's steel prison door, and now they have to pass an open one with only a guard between them and a convicted murderer.

Oba screams again, loud enough to make Richard's teeth vibrate. He slams into his cell door like a battering ram. The Hooded Men turn to see whether it's time to start running. Anton Leemaster and Madeline step toward Oba's cell. The third guard tries to move the Hooded Men along but they are frozen in front of Holabi Minco's open cell door.

"Hey there." Minco steps into the hallway. Extends an open hand to the executioners. Tribute?

Feathers. Owl feathers. Richard touches his shirt pocket. Feels the popsicle sticks Holabi Minco put there. Knows they are keeping company with a feather exactly like the ones Minco blows off of his palm.

The Hooded Men watch the cloud of feathers fly overhead and fall on them like a magic hailstorm. They run down the hallway toward the first set of locked double security doors, slapping at the feathers that have landed on them as if they were beating off a swarm of Africanized bees.

Anton Leemaster rushes back to Holabi Minco's cell, steps over the feathers as if they are cleverly disguised land mines. He draws his truncheon back, ready to swing at the magic man's face. Ready to leave a bloody bruise the inmate will take with him to the death chamber.

But Richard Harjo grabs his hand. "Not wise, Leemaster. Not wise at all."

The guard looks into Richard's eyes, like a coyote that's about to snatch the bait from a spring trap, but is having second thoughts.

Madeline scurries over the floor collecting the feathers while Anton Leemaster decides it's not a good idea to club a prison chaplain. Not good for his career. Not good for his soul. Not good for anything.

Holabi Minco puts a hand on Richard's shoulder. "The Lord works in mysterious ways, don't he, Rev?"

15

Oba Taylor stares at Richard through the reinforced glass window in his cell door. The spiraling sevens and swastika tattoos are distorted by the hate that twists the muscles around his eyes. His pupils have absorbed his irises like a pair of black holes.

Richard Harjo, PhD, sees an optical illusion caused by prison lighting, colored by fear. The Reverend Richard Harjo sees evil living inside a murderer's head. Still unable to decide which viewpoint is the right one.

Grandma Clementine told him it would be like this if he chose to get a secular education. She told him a holy man had to carry his own baggage on his walk with God, and an educated holy man has a lot of heavy baggage.

Richard wants to look away from Oba Taylor, but those dark eyes won't release their hold.

"Nothing stops a man like me." Taylor's breath steams the window. He draws a five-pointed star in the grey cloud. His black pupils show through the two lateral points of the pentagram.

H-Unit inmates are saturated with the magic of a certain death at a certain time in a certain way. They don't all believe in God but they all believe in something.

"Did Tammy tell you about me and her? Bet she didn't." Oba's lips stretch into an open mouthed smile. His tongue pokes at the gap where a central incisor used to be, reminding Richard of Earline. Oba's white sister.

"Me and Tammy and Burdette and Wolfie." The inmate wipes the viewing window free of fog. "That little redhead witched me into confessing, Rev. Injun preachers know about witchin', don't they?"

"Oba . . . ." Richard wants to talk about his visit to Grandma Angina's house, but he can't think how to start. Does Oba even know she's dead?

"What's that in your pocket, Rev?"

Richard thinks Oba is asking about the tortoise shell hair clips, but those are in the front seat of his car, still attached to Grandma Angina's hair.

"I'll bring them to you later, Oba." Richard looks back at Holabi Minco's cell. The owl feathers are gone. Anton Leemaster turns the key, spits on the floor. Says something nasty to Holabi though the speaking slots. Richard can't make out the words over Oba Taylor's noisy breathing, but he can tell by Leemaster's face the words have left a bitter taste.

"I'll have her." Anton Leemaster's voice is loud and clear he steps away from the cell and looks at a point on the wall halfway between Richard Harjo and Holabi Minco.

"I'll find her again," he says. "After you're dead, Holabi. Think about me and her when they slip the needle in."

"Kinta." Richard regrets saying the girl's name inside the prison walls, but it's too late to take it back.

Anton Leemaster turns toward him. Takes a step in his direction. Still holding his truncheon.

Another step toward Richard Harjo, slow and mechanical, like a locomotive rolling down a hill, sure to pick up speed as it heads for a disaster that can't be stopped.

"Not allowed to give the inmates nothing Rev. Not allowed to take nothing from them neither." He smacks the truncheon into the palm of his hand. Much too hard, but Anton Leemaster doesn't flinch.

Another step. "Better give it to me, Rev. Better let me see what that witch gave you." The pressure of the guard's attention settles on Richard Harjo's chest. Over the popsicle sticks in his shirt pocket.

Anton Leemaster smacks his palm again. "Might be a message, Rev. Might be a code message to that witchy daughter of his."

"It's nothing," Richard reaches for his pocket. "Part of a stick calendar." Covers the pocket with his hand like he's about to pledge allegiance to the flag.

Leemaster is within striking distance. Draws the truncheon back. "Show me."

Oba Taylor wipes the viewing window of his cell with his palm. "Whup him, Leemaster. I'm your witness."

Richard pulls the popsicle sticks out of his pocket. Three of them, like always.

"Whup the Injun preacher's ass," Oba Taylor says. "I'll say he started it."

Anton Leemaster considers the value of a witness like Oba Taylor for a second. It's enough to slow him down. He reaches for the popsicle sticks in Richard Harjo's hand.

"Class D felony to transport something like this, Rev." Leemaster smiles as he sorts through the sticks, looking for the message written in Holabi Minco's blood. Still has the truncheon, but maybe he won't need it now.

He turns the sticks over. The first is blank. Oba Taylor's name is written on the second. The third one has another name: Anton Leemaster.

The guard drops the sticks on the floor and backs all the way to the security double doors that lead out of H-Unit. Pounds on the glass until the first door slides open. Pounds on the second until the security team decides to let him pass.

"Good trick, Rev." Respect vibrates in Oba Taylor's voice. "Must have a little white blood in your veins."

"Everybody's got a little." Richard locks gazes with Oba Taylor. Holds it until he's sure the inmate understands his meaning. Then he walks away.

16

Madeline tells Richard, "Lorado Mendez wants to make a confession," as he reaches the double doors that will take him out of H-Unit.

"Not the kind that takes a lawyer," she says. "The religious kind, like Catholics do."

"I'm not a priest." It sounds like an apology. Richard wonders how many apologies he'll have to make before all is said and done. "Maybe I can get one to come here and talk to him."

"Need to see him today, Rev. Holabi says he's next to die."

Richard wants to tell her Oba's next, that Holabi's popsicle sticks don't matter. But they just saved him from a beating, so maybe he's wrong. Maybe he's been wrong about everything since he was ten years old.

"I lost Lorado's stick," Richard says.

"Don't matter Rev." Madeline takes him by the hand and pulls him toward Lorado Mendez's cell. "Once Holabi writes a man's name on the calendar he's doomed."

Lorado Mendez is on his knees as Richard enters his cell. Kneeling beside his bunk in the middle of a Spanish version of Hail Mary. "Santa Maria, Madre de Dios . . . ." He stops. Looks at Richard while he mouths the rest of his act of contrition silently . . . ruega por nosotros pecadores, ahora y en la hora de nuestra muerte. Amén.

Before Richard Harjo can stop himself, he makes the sign of the cross. Mumbles, "Spectacles, testicles, wallet and watch," the way he'd seen it done on Monty Python's Flying Circus and hopes Lorado thinks he's speaking Latin.

"They move us every time there's an execution," the inmate says without a trace of Mexico in his voice. "So I can't keep track of my Marias with scratches on the wall."

"Tried counting them on a paper but the guards take my notes every time there's a search." Lorado crosses himself. Tries to imitate Richard's Monty Python quote but loses his train of thought at "testicles."

"You've still got an appeal," Richard tells him. "Still got a chance."

Lorado says, "Concrete floor hurts my knees. Makes it hard to pray." Crosses himself again.

Richard starts to tell him God can hear him even if he's not kneeling, but maybe he can't. Maybe there are spiritual rules and regulations Richard didn't learn in seminary. Maybe owl feathers really are magic, and life and death really are decided by names on a popsicle stick calendar and Samantha's skeleton is lying underneath Burdette and Wolfie Lafleur's old house waiting to be properly buried.

"Can God forgive me if I killed a priest?"

"He can." Richard wonders if that's really true. Lorado Mendoza sees his doubt.

"Will he?" Lorado crosses himself again. His knees pop as he stands and looks at the ceiling. He asks if God can see through steel doors and cement walls into the heart of a priest killer in H-Unit. "Had a good reason, but maybe it wasn't good enough."

Richard wants to tell him God will forgive him for everything if he's sincere, but he can't put the words together.

"Act of contrition." Mendez puts a diphthong in the middle of contrition, Oklahoma style. "Hard to make one in a prison. How many Marias for a murdered priest?"

Richard wants to give him a number. Something he'll believe, because believing is the only thing Lorado Mendez has at this point. "Faith and mathematics don't really go together, Lorado." Of course there is the Trinity, and the twelve tribes of Israel, and the seven days it took to make the world but that's not math—at least Richard doesn't think so.

The inmate crosses himself again. He's been saying Hail Marys for almost a decade now and so far he doesn't feel forgiven. "Maybe if I had some holy water, Rev. From Saint Apolonia's—you know. Where it all happened."

"What the newspapers called the incident." Lorado doesn't make excuses. Doesn't say his victim "needed killin,'" the way Tammy Biggerstaff did.

"You ain't a priest, Rev, but maybe you're exactly what I need."

"Holy water from Saint Apolonia's." Richard wants to tell him holy water is superstitious nonsense—ordinary water, drawn from a faucet, poured into a marble stoup that's teeming with bacteria from hundreds of religious fingers—but he doesn't.

"And maybe a sign from the lady herself. I'd feel forgiven if I had a sign." Mendez crosses himself again. His lips move through another Ave Maria, asking for forgiveness from the head mistress of all the saints, assuming she's a multilingual lip reader.

Richard Harjo, PhD, wonders if all the crossing and Hail Marys have become a religious tick. A Catholic version of Tourette's Syndrome. He wonders if he could talk the prison medic into administering haloperidol or clonidine. But the Reverend Richard Harjo wonders if those drugs would limit Lorado's chance of absolution.

"I'll do what I can," he tells the inmate. "Sorry I lost your stick." He can see that Lorado Mendez doesn't have the slightest idea what he is talking about. "Where is Saint Apolonia's anyway?"

17

"Where are we going?"

Richard nearly faints when he hears Kinta speak to him from the back seat of his car.

"How . . . ?" He forgets his question as she scrambles over the backrest into the front. Finding women in the back seat of his car is happening way too often. At least Kinta won't ask him to drop her off at Nasty's Titty Bar.

"Back window's been shot out," she reminds him. "Sorry I didn't give you more warning about Oba's people."

Or any warning at all. Richard sort of knew what he was getting into. The marijuana field, bootlegging operation and meth lab were pretty good indicators. And it was Oba Taylor's family after all. He considers telling Kinta about Linda Sanchez for no more than a second.

"Quests have to be challenging." She points to the tortoise shell clips on the seat between them. "Something for Oba? To help him to the other side?"

"Oba Taylor needs all the help he can get." Richard steers his car to the exit of the prison employee parking lot. Waves to the guard who's supposed to control access. Kinta also waves to him as they pass through. The guard uses both hands to return the double wave, not a bit surprised to see her.

"Most everybody in Pittsburgh County's got a little Choctaw blood." She scoots close to the middle of the front seat. As close to Richard as Tammy Wynette Biggerstaff sat the day she marked his face. He doesn't want to look at Kinta's fingernails but he can't help himself.

"Your job usually stops at the parking lot, doesn't it Rev?" Her leg touches his. It's filled with heat and electricity, impossible to ignore. "Now it stretches a lot further."

Richard thinks about all the men who've been executed on his watch. All the men and the one woman he walked into the death chamber and told about the benevolent God waiting for them on the other side of H-Unit's concrete walls. He thinks about the endless line of murderers yet to come.

Grandma Clementine told him, "The worst sinners need help the most," after she came home from witnessing his father's execution. "Prayin' on the wrong side of the glass didn't help my Richard none," she said. "And the prison chaplain didn't take it serious."

A horn brings Richard's attention back to the road. He's nearly crossed over the yellow line. Nearly ran into an oncoming car. He wants to tell Kinta Minco he doesn't know what his job is anymore. Where it starts. Where it stops. Maybe he never did. But all Richard can do at the moment is think about what it's like to drive a car with no back window and Holabi Minco's daughter in the front seat.

Pretty girl. Kinta fills his mind. Pushes out memories of Grandmother Clementine, and his father.

Pretty girl, like Anton Leemaster said. A really pretty girl who's chosen to sit next to Richard Harjo for reasons he can't understand and doesn't really want to. Richard drives by a police car hidden behind a red cedar tree. Sees its lights come on. Sees it lurch forward as the policeman inside shifts it into gear.

"Reckless driving." Richard wants to say something better than that. Something Kinta Minco will think is clever, but she's not paying attention to him right now. She's waving to the police car. Smiling at the traffic cop through a rear window that's been shot out by Oba Taylor's people while Richard was on a quest to help a racist murderer die more easily.

The police car pulls over to the side of the road again and stops. Bewitched by Kinta Minco. Richard understands completely. He's bewitched too. In the power of something completely natural and also something that feels completely supernatural as he drives his bullet-riddled car to the house where Tammy Biggerstaff took "naked whuppins" and where she killed her lesbian lover and left her body in the crawl space.

"Lorado Mendez . . . ." The Reverend Richard Harjo remembers the promises he made: Holy water, a sign from The Lady. Maybe he'll keep those promises after he visits Samantha's bones.

The promise to Samantha comes first. That promise was made to a ghost inside a tunnel that led straight to the afterlife—if it wasn't a hallucination caused by secretions of an oxygen-starved gland in the center of his brain. Either way, Richard has to know for sure.

He feels tears trickling down his cheeks. Doesn't know exactly why he's crying. There are so many reasons: lost souls he was supposed to save, loss of the faith that was supposed to guide his life. He flinches when Kinta Minco captures a tear on a fingertip and tastes it.

"You're a good man, Richard Harjo." As if the flavor of his tears has told her everything she needs to know. "A real good man for a preacher."

He hasn't the slightest idea what she means by that and he doesn't care. As long as Kinta is willing to sit beside him as he pulls into the gravel driveway of a house he's seen once before, when he was holding hands with a murderer, looking at it from the end of a dark tunnel with Tammy's dead lover pointing the way.

"Holabi tried to leave you out of it Rev," Kinta tells him. "Tried to work it out another way." She looks into Richard's eyes long enough to make him squirm and then turns her attention to the house.

"What will we find here?" She hasn't got enough magic to read his mind. This is his quest. His mission. Arranged by Tammy and Samantha and maybe Holabi Minco to do something that has to be done by a holy man.

A holy man who hasn't made his mind up about the supernatural yet, but if things turn out as he thinks they might . . . .

"Bones," he tells her. "But first I want to look inside the house."

18

Shotgun shack. That's what people in this part of Oklahoma call houses like this one. The front door and the back door line up so straight a shotgun blast can pass through uninterrupted. At least it could have until someone got busy with a hammer and nails and plasterboard and paint. Until someone filled the house with desperate little rooms no bigger than cells on H-Unit.

"Good place for a killer to live," Richard says. "Good practice for Death Row."

The front was broken open long ago, but if it hadn't been, Richard Harjo would have kicked it in. He couldn't turn away from his quest now that Kinta was with him, watching him, approving of him, believing in him one hundred percent.

When a girl like Kinta Minco is with a man, he'll do most anything she wants. Like smuggling envelopes to death row inmates, and visiting the family home of a rabid racist killer, and whatever else she might think of.

Kinta takes hold of his hand—his Tammy hand—and Richard feels electricity run up his arm. Enough to charge his religious batteries to do whatever task God or Holabi Minco has set before him.

It doesn't take long for him to find the room where Tammy killed her lover. Perspective is different at ground level. Time is different. Everything is older, more run down. The paint has flaked a little more. Mold has done more damage to the plasterboard. He sees stains on the floor where Samantha's blood pooled before it seeped through the tongue-and-groove joints of the pine floor and leaked onto the dirt in the crawl space where her bones are lying now.

Probably.

"The baseboard is loose here." Kinta lets go of Richard's hand and points. All the baseboards are warped and displaced but one has pulled away from the wall at least an inch.

Richard sees circular depressions in the pine floor-planks that match the legs of the iron bed where Tammy and Samantha made love. The bed is gone, but he sees a dream image of it, almost solid enough to touch.

Kinta is on her knees, pulling at the baseboard. Insects run across the floor. The smell of rodent urine taints the air. She teases a wooden box inlayed with a crucifixion scene out of the space inside the wall. The finish has been clouded by moisture, gnawed by mice. An ebony cross wobbles in the red oak top. A cubist Jesus is nailed to it with giant surrealistic spikes. A squarish Roman Centurion thrusts a spear into his side. Supernatural cruelty. Symbolic of punished innocence. The foundation of a religion that includes the Golden Rule.

"Was Jesus' name written on the Roman equivalent of a popsicle stick?" Richard asks without expecting an answer.

"Best not dwell on that." Kinta works the latch on the front of the box. The hinges creak like the cell doors in H-Unit. She lifts out a double-edged dagger with a grip made of alternating onyx and brass cylinders. The blade is rust free but has a fine patina of dried blood. Juarez, Mexico is engraved at the base of the blade where it joins the hilt.

"Samantha's blood," Richard says. "One more thing it's best not to dwell on."

"There are pictures too." Kinta shows him photos. The paper is yellowed but the images are plain. Burdette and Wolfie Lafleur—the two men with shaved heads from the witness room at Tammy Biggerstaff's execution. Tammy is posed between them as if she's being restrained. They are smiling; she is not. Her eyes are focused on something far away, perhaps a future time when she's beyond their reach.

There's a picture of Samantha in the box. And one of Oba Taylor before he had the facial tattoos. Hard to recognize, but the hateful expression on his face is unmistakable.

"Oba?" Richard's hand goes to his shirt pocket where Oba Taylor's popsicle stick used to rest beside Anton Leemaster's. Gone. He remembers watching

Leemaster drop them on the floor. Didn't pick them up because that would be like admitting he believed in magic. "What's his picture doing here?"

He remembers Oba Taylor talking to him through the H-Unit cell door: "Did Tammy tell you about me and her? I'll bet she didn't. Me and Tammy and Burdette and Wolfie Lafleur."

"There aren't so many murderers in Oklahoma," Kinta says. "Less than doctors, less than preachers, a lot less than lawyers. Killers hang together when they can."

Richard knows that is true. Murderers shake hands, trade cigarettes and secrets when they are coming up through the penal system where they graduate from burglary, to robbery, to assault with intent to kill, to going all the way. Richard's father was on a first-name basis with all the famous murderers of his day by the time he selected his last meal.

Oklahoma killers shared legal strategies and attorneys. Scratched their names on the same cell walls in H-Unit as they worked their way to the death chamber. Eventually the murderers went to the same county morgue and were buried in the same prison graveyard.

"Let's look under the house." Richard heads for the door while Kinta shoves the box back into its hiding place. He doesn't bother to explain about Samantha's bones because they still have a chance of being a side effect of hallucinogenic secretions of his pineal body. Or a shared death experience, no more authentic than a sympathetic pregnancy or a contact high.

19

The house is supported by rectangular cement pylons. The spaces between the footings have been bricked over with salvaged paving stone and low quality quickset mortar that has mostly turned to sand. Gaps in the stone barrier allow for easy passage for Richard and for animals. He wonders if there'll be anything left of Samantha—if she was ever really there.

This part of Oklahoma is rural enough for coyotes and urban enough for stray dogs. Samantha's bones could be spread all over Pittsburgh County by now but Richard thinks they probably aren't. Her ghost is too quiet to attract the notice of policemen but too scary for coyotes and dogs.

He sees the skeleton, pristine white in a beam of sunlight that points through a hole in the house's crumbling skirt. Samantha's bones are picked clean by ants and beetles bleached by their digestive juices. Spider webs cover the orbits of the skull and the mandible. They tie ribs to the vertebrae, attach carpals to metacarpals to phalanges.

"Hello, Samantha." Richard knows she won't answer but her ghost will expect a greeting.

"I'll get you out of here," he tells her. Speaking as if he believes her ghost is listening. Conversing with the dead the way holy men have always done, but psychologists think is crazy.

Richard almost believes Samantha is talking to him, mumbling in a low butch voice then moving up the scale to a more feminine pitch. He listens for a while, tries to make out words, but can't. Because the words are not coming from the skeleton. They are coming from outside the house. Beyond the stone barrier where he left Kinta.

Kinta's and a man's voice, getting louder, revving up into an argument.

"Thought nobody lived here," Kinta says. "Thought maybe it was for rent."

Richard watches through an irregular square hole where the bricks have fallen inside. He waits to see how effective Kinta's lie is going to be.

"Yes," she tells the man. "I'm here alone."

Richard has seen him twice before. Once in the witness room of the execution chamber before Tammy Biggerstaff flew him to the frontier of Heaven, and once in a yellowed photograph inside a box hidden in the wall of the room where Samantha was murdered.

Now Burdette Lafleur is standing outside a house where he lived with his son and his stepdaughter and had his photo taken with Oba Taylor. Now he's with Kinta. Another pretty girl with no one near who'll stand up for her. Richard watches the smile take shape on Lafleur's face as he conjures up mental images of "naked whuppin's."

"All alone." Burdette Lafleur waves to someone behind the steering wheel of a red Silverado pickup truck that's parked behind Richard's car in the gravel drive. The driver answers Burdette's wave with a snappy military salute.

Richard has seen him before too. Wolfie Lafleur. The skinhead who sat beside his father at Tammy's execution. The man who shot out Richard's back window as he sped away from the Patch with Linda Sanchez in his back seat.

Two skinheads against a Creek preacher and a Choctaw girl. Not good odds.

Burdette surveys the house, the trees around the house, he checks out Richard Harjo's car with no back windshield and spider cracks circling bullet holes in the front.

"Injun car." He spits on the ground so Kinta will know he doesn't like the taste of the word.

"Injun girl." He doesn't spit this time, because the idea of a pretty, helpless Indian girl tastes sweet. He rotates three hundred sixty degrees before he considers the consequences for what he might do to this pretty Choctaw girl who's all alone where she has no business being.

"Nobody comes around here much no more. Not me. Not my boy. Not Injun girls lookin' for a place to squat." His hands spread out like a pair of giant spiders. They settle on his jeans. They creepy crawl up his legs, and stop when they reach his belt. They find their way to the buckle and start the work of unfastening it, slow and steady with no help from Burdette's eyes that are both locked on Kinta in case she's smart enough to run.

His conversation sounds harmless as his hands move according to their own agenda. Kinta takes a backward step, tenses for a sprint or a fight, whichever seems best when Burdette finally decides whether his conversation or his hands are going to carry the day.

Richard hears the sound of Wolfie's pickup door popping open. Burdette's boy stays inside. Still hasn't decided whether to join in. He's interested. Richard is sure of that. Wolfie's seen his dad in action before, wouldn't mind seeing him again.

And he will, if things go as Burdette and Wolfie think they will. Richard has met too many murderers to have any doubt how things are supposed to work out.

Burdette will have his way with Kinta, and Wolfie will come for what he leaves behind. Maybe they'll kill her. Maybe they'll let her live. They haven't thought that far ahead. Opportunistic killers never do.

Richard places his hands on the edges of the square hole in the brick barrier and charges forward. He screams—shrill as a teenage girl but powerful as a Viking berserker—almost a shriek, but without the edge of fear. Richard breaks through the wall like a lineman driving toward a quarterback. He comes away with a brick in each hand, stumbles as he straightens up, but not before he winds up and throws a paving brick at Burdette Lafleur.

Burdette tries to step aside but his hands have loosened his belt. His pants slide down to mid thigh level, contain his stride enough to keep him within the target zone. The brick catches him on the ear. Takes a piece as it bounces off his temple. A mist of blood speckles Kinta's face.

Like Tammy Biggerstaff's freckles.

Burdette Lafleur must think so too, because he calls Tammy's name.

Richard falls onto the gravel driveway, rolls quickly so Burdette can't jump on him. He scrambles to his feet and throws the second brick at the Chevy Silverado.

Wild pitch. Not even close. Wolfie pulls the door to the truck closed, and starts the engine. Burdette Lafleur pulls up his pants and kicks Richard in the stomach, so hard he crumples into a ball of pain.

Richard barely feels it when Lafleur kicks him in the mouth, but he tastes the blood and he feels the weight of the larger slick-headed man sitting on his chest.

"Wolfie!" Burdette calls to his son, who still hasn't joined in the fight.

Richard doesn't waste time wondering why. He rakes his fingernails across Lafleur's face—a Tammy Biggerstaff strategy—so the two men have matching wounds. One fresh and bloody and one scabbed over like time-lapse photographs of impotent rage.

They roll across the driveway in front of the house where Samantha's bones are waiting to be buried. The gravel is all points and sharp edges. When they come to a stop Richard is on bottom, but he takes hold of Burdette's shirt with one hand and breaks the skinhead's nose with the other. He thinks of Asian holy men who preach nonviolence and study martial arts.

Richard knows he should be throwing punches instead of thinking about Kung Fu, especially when he is lying on his back with Burdette Lafleur on top of him.

"I know you," Burdette Lafleur's right hand has found the paving brick that mutilated his ear. His fingers slip in the blood while he gets a killing grip.

"You're the preacher was with Tammy." He brings the brick high enough to crush Richard Harjo's skull. He means to crush Richard Harjo's skull, but drops the brick behind him.

Compassion? Some murderers are compassionate men. Richard doesn't think Burdette is one of those.

Lafleur wobbles to his feet, stands over Richard legs spread, pants falling to his knees. He reaches over his shoulder with his left hand. Reaches around his back with his right. Like a man with an itch in an unreachable place.

Burdette Lafleur had forgotten about Kinta for a while. Richard forgot her too. They both remember when she says, "How's that feel, Burdette?"

Richard is on his feet trying to figure out what stopped Burdette Lafleur from killing him. He sees the knife in Lafleur's back as the skinhead staggers down the driveway like a bit player in a Zombie movie.

Tammy's knife, the one she used on Samantha.

"Thought it might come in handy." Kinta follows Burdette Lafleur, as graceful as a ballet dancer moving across the stage. He turns and menaces her with impotent threatening gestures, like a tarantula that's watching a cowboy boot getting ready to descend.

She kicks Burdette in the groin. Watches him crumple to all fours, like reverse evolution. Before he can crawl away she snatches the knife and wipes the blade on his shirt.

Burdette shouts, "Jesus," more like he's looking for someone to blame than pleading for divine assistance. He struggles to his feet again. Walks backwards so he can keep an eye on Kinta, who he finally understands is the most dangerous pretty girl he's ever encountered. Bloody circles spread under his arms and meet over his navel.

Burdette calls on Jesus again, but it comes out, "Cheese." As if he's trying to mitigate taking the Lord's name in vain, one baby step at a time.

"Think he'll die?" Kinta watches the big man holding his pants up with one hand as he backs down the gravel drive.

"Probably not." Richard looks at the handful of Burdette's shirt still in his hand. Uses it to wipe the blood off of his lips.

He spits on the ground, wiggles a loose tooth with his tongue, tosses the rag onto the gravel.

"There's something inside it." Kinta nudges the bloody fragment of Burdette's ruined shirt with her shoe.

"Dog tags." She lifts the tags by the broken chain. Dangles them in front of Richard until he takes them from her. "Burdette was a Gulf War veteran."

Richard shouts, "Thank you for your service, asshole," at Burdette Lafleur as he takes the dog tags from Kinta. He walks to the house. Looks through the hole he just broke through. Tosses in the dog tags. He thinks he hears them bounce off of Samantha's skeleton. He can't be sure, but they'll be close enough for the police to find.

"Got a cell phone?" he asks Kinta. "I need to report a murder."

20

It doesn't take Wolfie Lafleur very long to pick sides in a fight. His old habits kick in and he's already jacking a bullet into his pistol, ready to charge out of his truck and put things right. White people win; muddy people lose. Like it says in the Good Book.

But when Wolfie gets a look at these two muddy people, he freezes solid.

"Holy crapola." The low-watt swear words are embarrassing, but Kinta makes everything Wolfie's been sure of all his life hop around like words on a printed page.

By the time his mind figures out what to do, his body has already made a decision. Wolfie Lafleur watches himself slide his pistol under the seat of his Chevy Silverado and put his key into the ignition. It's like one of those out-of-body experiences he's seen on the SciFi channel.

His poison ivy brings him back to reality. It's already blossomed into full-fledged blisters that calamine lotion won't touch. He slaps the itchiest spot on his leg, but that makes the itching spread.

Wolfie figures the rash is some kind of Old Testament punishment for the sin he's about to commit. It's a pretty big deal to leave your daddy bleeding on a gravel driveway. Probably a cardinal sin—whatever that is.

Since he can't ask Burdette for advice, he closes his eyes and tips his head up so he can beam his thoughts straight to God.

He wants to ask if Kinta's presence is some kind of sign.

And what it means.

And what he's supposed to do next.

But even God is having a hard time figuring this one out. Wolfie waits for a voice to boom out of the sky like it does in movies about the old time Bible days. But things never go that way for Wolfie.

According to Burdette Lafleur, a son is supposed to, "Honor thy father and thy mother," and when dad chases mom away all the surplus honor falls to the parent who's still around. Burdette explained it all to Wolfie this afternoon. He used his inside voice and lots of big words, so he'd come across reasonable and scholarly. When Wolfie showed signs of doubt Burdette fetched his Holy Bible—the one he ordered special from Kansas City with *Burdette Lafleur* pressed into the vinyl cover and painted to look like gold.

Daddy flopped the Good Book open to a page filled with red sentences. He ran his finger underneath a line and recited the holy words in the deepest most religious voice he could muster.

Burdette was hard to ignore when he talked like that. And the biblical words he touched with the tip of his finger were the deepest red of any on the page. When Wolfie saw that holy red color all he could think about was the morning sun shining through the eastern window of Kinta Minco's Jack Fork house.

Wolfie pretended he could read the words as Burdette pointed them out, but all he did was repeat whatever his daddy said. He threw in a halleluiah or two whenever he stumbled. When the halleluiahs piled up too deep, he spoke in tongues. A man has to show respect for red words in the Bible.

Red is the most important color in the world. The color of blood, the color of the planet Mars, the color of Wolfie's Chevy Silverado, the color of the fire in Burdette Lafleur's eyes when somebody crosses him. Like when his only son doesn't want to drive his pickup truck down the road that leads to their old house and check up on the car that drove that way thirty minutes earlier.

"Not much down there," Burdette said. "Except for our old place."

That wasn't exactly true. There were lots of abandoned houses, and an illegal dumpsite, and a place where half-breed teenage boys go to huff paint and suck the nitrous oxide propellant out of stolen cans of whipping cream.

Burdette had a hunch the car he saw was headed to their old house. He also had a hunch there was a woman in the car. Wolfie knew his daddy had a way with hunches.

"If it's a muddy boy we'll whip his ass. If it's a muddy girl we'll whip her ass and then . . . ."

Wolfie didn't feel like this was a very good day for ass whuppin' or rape. He was still thinking about the Indian girl he saw when he woke up from an ecstasy coma. Prettiest girl on the planet earth. Nicest too.

Wolfie Lafleur was in love for sure. The deepest, hardest, most serious kind of muddy love.

"Poison ivy's put me out of the mood," Wolfie told his dad. But the truth was, it was Kinta Minco who put him out of the mood for gang rape. Especially going at it with his daddy, who was also his spiritual advisor, and also the biggest asshole in Oklahoma.

Wolfie starts his truck and shifts it into reverse. If God wants to stop him he can make the clutch slip or lock the emergency brake.

He gives the Lord a few seconds to decide what he's going to do, then backs out the driveway.

Burdette staggers toward the truck way too slow to catch up. His nose is broken, his pants have settled around his ankles and what's left of his ripped up shirt has soaked up about all the blood it can hold. Daddy looks pretty bad, but Wolfie figures he'll be all right. A man will always be all right if God is on his side.

The truth is, Wolfie likes the Injun girl a lot more than he ever liked Burdette. She was kind to him, like his daddy never was. Pulled his white ass out of the forest. Nursed him back to consciousness with herbal tea, then pointed him toward the Patch and gave him a shove. Like he was one of those drone missiles the government uses to kill Arabs.

Couldn't expect her to keep him. Wasn't logical, as that pointy-eared guy on Star Trek used to say. Not with his white power tattoos and him telling her all about Linda Sanchez when his head was still spinning and his mind wasn't clear.

The preacher is another matter. He'd been nice to Tammy, but he stole Linda Sanchez before Wolfie could catch her alone.

Now it looks like the holy man is sweet on Kinta, and maybe she's sweet on him too.

Wolfie stops the truck and weighs the pros and cons of going back. He's got a full clip of bullets for his nine millimeter pistol. Plenty for the preacher, but he figures Kinta might not like watching her boyfriend take a bullet.

Best to try and break this Injun girl the gentle way. With as little bloodshed as possible, and none of it hers.

21

Lorado Mendez is on his knees again, adding to his tally of Ave Marias. Alternating Spanish with English. This is something new.

Richard sets a mason jar of water on the floor and sits on the cement bunk while Lorado makes his case with Jesus's mother.

The pant legs of Mendez' jumpsuit are pulled up past the knees so he'll suffer more as he begs forgiveness for killing a man who molested children left in his care.

"Reckon the padre's burning in hell, Rev." Lorado struggles to his feet, massages his knees where the rough concrete surface has penetrated the skin. His eyes pause for a moment on Richard's swollen lips and his black eye and then get back to their search for God.

"So tell me what happened, Rev?"

Richard fiddles with his loose premolar. It's not as sore as yesterday but it's a lot looser.

"Little scuffle at a crime scene." It's easy to slip into a lie when you are ashamed of framing a man for murder. Even a man like Burdette Lafleur who needs killing as much as any man who ever lived.

"Got some information from an inmate." He repeats the story he told the police. "Given to me in my capacity as his religious advisor. Wants to remain anonymous . . . you know how it goes." Richard has been telling religious lies for over a decade now. What harm could another do?

Breaking the ninth commandment is getting to be easy for Richard Harjo. It's pretty low on the hierarchy of cardinal sins. One above greed; one below stealing. He thinks about the stolen tortoise shell hair clips in his pocket. Maybe he should follow Lorado Mendez's example, pull up his pant legs and get down on his knees.

Lorado mumbles another Hail Mary while Richard wonders if his story has any holes the police will figure out later on. He fiddles with his loose tooth and tries to think of a half-truth or two that will fill in the gaps.

"Found a skeleton," he tells Lorado. "Called the cops. Looks like Burdette Lafleur killed somebody a long time ago." Careful not to say too much because complicated lies break down quickly.

Lorado sits on his cement bunk, massages his knees. Picks little bits of sand out of the skin. "I mean what happened at Saint Apolonia's, Rev? Looks like you got the holy water."

Another lie Richard doesn't want to bog down with too much detail.

"Sure thing." He never had a toothache before today. It feels better when he bites on it. The premolar hits harder than it used to, and it hurts, but it hurts in a good way that takes his mind off of all the things he's done.

The water in the jar came from Richard's kitchen tap. Moderated by a Britta filter instead of a priest's blessing. Richard tried to pray over it but the best he could come up with was, "Please bless this water for Lorado, OK?" Didn't bother to say amen.

Richard isn't sure where Saint Apolonia's is. McAlester maybe. Possibly Tulsa. He fills up the silence in the H-Unit cell with words so Lorado Mendez won't pick up on the fact that even though Richard Harjo has been telling the same sort of religious lies for almost ten years now, he isn't very good at it.

"You've said plenty of Hail Marys," Richard says. "Anything over a thousand is bonus miles." It hurts when Richard smiles, partly because he's pushing his smile up a mountain of untruth and partly because his loose premolar has worked half out of the socket and there's no comfortable way to hold his mouth.

The pain kept him awake most of the night and when he finally got to sleep he dreamed he went to Saint Apolonia's and the priest told him it was time he stopped lying to everyone and start figuring out who he is.

Lorado Mendez looks like he doesn't believe anything Richard has said. He looks like he's thinking about getting on his knees again and starting in on a new series of Hail Marys. But first he puts a fingertip in the mason jar of water. He touches it to his tongue, samples its holiness.

Richard doesn't think the water is going to pass inspection, and his tooth is getting really loose, and it's hurting more than ever, so he reaches into his mouth and pulls it out. Rips it free as quickly as he can, the way he'd pull a Band-Aid off of a hairy arm.

It's amazingly pain-free. He holds the tooth in his fingers. Watches a drop of blood roll off the bifurcated root and drip on the floor where Lorado Mendez just got finished saying his last Hail Mary.

Another drop of blood is ready to fall, but Mendez catches it. Dips a finger in the holy water again. Mixes it with the blood in the palm of his hand. Uses the finger to paint a cross on his forehead in diluted preacher blood.

"My sign," Lorado Mendez says.

Richard's toothache is gone. The place where the tooth used to be feels hot and salty, but there is no pain at all. He wants to tell Lorado the extracted tooth is no sign from God. It's just a gap in a preacher's smile that will have to be filled in by a dentist.

"Saint Apolonia was a martyr, Rev." Lorado takes the premolar from Richard's fingers and clasps it against his heart.

"Romans tortured her by pulling out her teeth," he says, because it's clear to him that Richard knows nothing about Saint Apolonia, or martyrs, or the Catholic Church.

"Wasn't sure you was a real holy man, Rev. Not till I saw the sign. Now there ain't no doubt." He sits in silence, holding the tooth, looking at it every now and then to make sure his miracle hasn't evaporated the way his holy water will eventually if he leaves the jar uncapped.

Lorado doesn't lip synch Hail Marys. Doesn't cross himself. "An absolute state of grace," he tells Richard Harjo. "Nothing I can do now to make things better."

Richard thinks he should be saying, Bless you my son, but he checks his watch instead. Follows the second hand around the numbers on the dial. His alarm sounds for no particular reason. Another sign from God?

"That means I've got to go," he says, even though it means no such thing. Richard Harjo knows his alarm is going off because it was accidentally set in a fight with Burdette Lafleur.

"Got to go see Oba Taylor," Richard says. "He's next to go."

"Maybe he is," Lorado Mendez says, "or maybe he ain't."

Richard stands at the viewing window of Lorado Mendez's cell and taps until Madeline comes to let him out.

"You look like hell, Rev," she tells him.

"Worn out from carrying signs from God," he tells her. "It's heavy work."

22

"Too many Moving Days this month." Madeline wants Richard to meet with Oba Taylor in the Waiting Room.

"He's been acting kind of strange," she says, as if Oba Taylor ever acted any other way. "This time tomorrow Oba will be out of this world. Most of him anyway." Madeline looks toward Holabi Minco's cell.

"The Choctaw double soul." Richard reads her thoughts like they were a large print version of a psychic how-to manual. He knows her background. Knows the belief system that shaped her mind. Watches for her tells, the way old school mystics have done for thousands of years and new-agers have figured out only recently.

"Oba's family wants his body," Madeline says. "Most don't."

"Wonder what they'll do with his bones?" She breaks eye contact. Looks at the floor while they walk past the corridor that leads to the shower room where Oba Taylor is being drenched with DOC water for the very last time.

Richard stops and nods to the four guards standing outside the shower room door. Four men he doesn't recognize, borrowed from general population because Oba is too scary for the usual three—especially when one of the usual guards is a woman.

"Anton's in there watching him," Madeline says. "He's got the most white blood. Oba won't mind being naked in front of Anton."

"White man's burden." Richard imagines the jailhouse ink covering parts of Oba's body he hasn't seen. More swastikas, and Christian Identity symbols. Tributes to Grandma. Oba's name plus some forgotten girlfriend's inside a blurry red heart.

Madeline tries to nudge him toward the Waiting Room, but Richard is in no hurry to visit that place again.

"Four guards instead of two," he says. Twice the usual back up for a final shower. They don't make jokes the way guards usually do on Moving Day, because Oba Taylor's inside, bellowing like a hippo in full rut.

"Shock sticks." Richard looks at the battery-powered wands. Usually truncheons are enough to subdue a naked inmate, but nobody's taking any chances with Oba.

"Anton's got one too," Madeline tells Richard. "Don't know what they'll do in a shower. Maybe kill a man. Maybe kill both men." They are hoping the threat of death is enough to keep Oba out of attack mode.

"He'll die tomorrow anyway." Richard remembers how Oba's name looked on the popsicle stick. Even letters, full of bloody flourishes. Like Anton Leemaster's name looked, only shorter.

The guards outside the shower know all about Holabi's stick calendar. Tales of witchcraft travel through the prison system as fast as news of a child molester in general population.

"Rumor is the Hooded Men won't come back." Richard hasn't heard any rumors about the executioners but he starts one now. The guards believe him the way children believe stories about flying reindeer.

"They're afraid Holabi Minco has figured out who they are." Richard says this as if he knows it for a certainty. Says it with the confidence of a man who has a pocket full of owl feathers.

Once Richard plants the rumor, the guards will tend it and make it grow. Holabi Minco writes a man's name on popsicle sticks. He puts them in the chaplain's pocket. Nobody knows how magic works, but a chain of holy men looks like witchcraft, and Richard Harjo looks more like a witch with every mark that shows up on his face.

"We heard about the skeleton you found," Madeline says. "The girl Burdette Lafleur killed."

The guards outside the shower room settle their eyes on the floor, grip their shock sticks tighter, and strain to hear the conversation between Richard and

Madeline. They know about Samantha's skeleton all right. They know he was with Kinta Minco when he found the girl. They've heard how Burdette's boy drove off and left him bleeding. How Burdette was easy for the cops to find because he left a trail of blood.

They glance at the bruises on Richard's face and look away.

"Lafleur almost died of his wounds." Richard's way of telling them, You ought to see the other guy.

The male guards trade glances. Make a point of not looking at Madeline. They've heard that Kinta went home with Richard Harjo. Spent the night with him. Disappeared before he woke up this morning.

Richard sees from the nervous way the guards shift their weight from one foot to the other, they got the facts from someone they trust. Someone who has been looking for Kinta since she stopped talking to her father in Choctaw through visitation telephones.

Did she put her hand on the glass barrier and feel the family connection through the half inch of insulated distance separating them? The way Richard did with his father. The connection that started Richard Harjo down the road that led him to this spot in front of the shower room where the guards are looking at the envelope protruding from his back pocket. An envelope with Kinta's name written on the front.

The letter "K" is all they can see for sure, but the guards are full of Native American Blood and they can guess the rest. No one tells him it's a class D felony to bring an envelope to a death row inmate. The guards are afraid of what else Richard Harjo might have in his pockets.

23

Anton Leemaster walks backward down the H-Unit hallway, leading Oba Taylor but not willing to turn his back on the mixed-race white supremacist. Richard stands in front of the Waiting Room and watches the procession.

Shackles limit Taylor's stride but he gradually closes the distance between himself and Leemaster. Four guards follow the prisoner like geese in a migratory flight. Everyone in the miniature parade is armed with shock sticks except for the inmate, but Oba looks more dangerous than all of them combined. Even in the robin's-egg-blue jumpsuit he'll wear to his execution, and then to the medical examiner's autopsy table in the Pittsburgh County Morgue, and probably to the makeshift table in the Patch where his body will be viewed by a collection of mourners who will look strikingly similar to the patrons in the bar scene in the very first episode of Star Wars.

Burying clothes. The Oklahoma Department of Corrections recycles everything except execution jumpsuits. Too much bad Karma is soaked into the cloth to be mixed with other items in the prison laundry. Burning is the only way. Cremation. Eighteen hundred degrees Fahrenheit—nine hundred eighty two degrees Celsius—turns soft tissue and bad Karma into smoke, reduces bones to ghost-free ashes.

Oba Taylor won't go up in smoke. He'll be hauled to the Patch in the bed of a cousin's rusty pickup truck, boxed in a DOC pine coffin that will collapse around his body in a matter of months and allow graveyard dirt to cover his white supremacist tattoos. What will the worms think of that?

No embalming fluid to slow them down. Oklahoma Taxpayers won't spend money to preserve the body of a killer. The ME might make a Y-incision in Oba's chest so he can weigh and dissect the internal organs or he might write lethal injection on the death certificate. Cause of death is never a mystery in the execution chamber.

Richard steps into the freshly-cleaned Waiting Room. He walks over to the stainless steel sink and washes his hands the way restaurant employees are supposed to after restroom visits. The way Pontius Pilot did before he sentenced Jesus.

You're part of this, Rev.

The chaplain lathers his hands with the alkaline bar of prison soap, knowing that some things can't be scrubbed away. His back is turned to the Waiting Room door but he hears the entourage stop. The chains on Oba Taylor's shackles make a noise like ice cubes bumping the sides of a glass as Anton Leemaster frees the prisoner's legs.

Richard turns and watches the ritual, his hands still wet, because the custodial team forgot to stock the Waiting Room with paper towels.

"Step into the cell." The guards hold their shock sticks in the present arms position like soldiers in a military parade. Anton Leemaster shuts the door and tells Oba to put his hands through the pass-through.

"'Less you want to eat your last meal in cuffs." After a minimum of fiddling, the inmate's hands are free. He stares at Leemaster through the viewing window. His face isn't reflected in the glass but his tattoos are. Backward swastika, backward-spiraling sevens, but the number 88 on Oba's forehead is unchanged. The numerical tribute to Hitler is a palindrome.

It's Richard Harjo's job to give condemned prisoners a chance to make their peace with God. Usually they have something to say the day before they walk the last mile. It's their final chance to make a good impression in case there's a spiritual recruiter watching from the sky who might decide they are ready for salvation.

Richard tells them Heaven is full of murderers and rapists who changed their ways one day before they were executed. It's a lucky religious technicality, like the wrong address on a search warrant. Saint Peter stands at the Pearly Gates holding a torch like the Statue of Liberty, welcoming the wretched criminal masses yearning to be free—as long as they die shortly after a sincere apology.

Oba Taylor doesn't act like he's ready to say he's sorry.

"If you can't remember this, write it down," the inmate tells Anton Leemaster. "Porter house steak, nearly burned. Fried potatoes, nearly burned. Cherry pie. Chocolate ice cream on the same plate but don't let 'em touch." He holds eye contact with the guard long enough to be sure he is ready for the most important part of the last meal order. "Plastic knife and fork will be okay, but I want something special for my napkin." He bumps his forehead against the window for emphasis. "Tammy Biggerstaff's panties is what I want. The ones she wore before her last shower. I know when the laundry gets done, so don't tell me it ain't possible."

Not exactly what Richard was expecting. Not what Anton Leemaster was expecting either. The guard doesn't say he'll have to check on that. Doesn't recommend a side from Geraldine's Restaurant. The word panties starts to take shape on his lips but he catches himself in time.

Richard Harjo is almost nine feet from Oba Taylor. As much distance as he can find inside the Waiting Room. He backs against the wall and pushes. Pretends it's possible to gain another inch.

Taylor turns away from the viewing window. Spreads his arms as if he's preparing to crush the world.

Oba means bear. Richard wishes he'd never thought of that.

Anton Leemaster has recovered from his prisoner's last meal order. He watches through the viewing window like a man in the front row of a strip bar with a pocket full of five-dollar bills. He licks his lips and smiles. "Have fun with your new girlfriend, Taylor."

The inmate rubs his wrists, where the restraints used to be. Flexes his fingers into fists covered with white supremacist ink and the—apparently mandatory—LOVE, HATE tats on his knuckles made famous by Richard Speck, an old time mass murderer Oba Taylor has probably never heard of.

"I don't fuck Injuns." Oba inhales so deeply, Richard is afraid he will suck every bit of air out of the room.

"But you do. Don't you Rev? I can smell her on you." Oba pops his knuckles. Throws his shoulders back, which makes him seem to grow a couple of inches taller, temporarily blocking Anton Leemaster's view.

Richard's right hand strays to the envelope in his back pocket with Kinta's name on it. Holabi Minco's name too. He considers saying those names to see what effect they have on Oba Taylor. To see if there's any magic in those names that will penetrate the inmate's Nazi-tattoo-armor.

Richard Harjo definitely feels fear as Oba Taylor steps his way, but mostly he feels Anton Leemaster watching from the safe side of the viewing window. The guard's voice finds its way around Oba Taylor: "Kinta and Harjo sitting in a tree. K-I-S-S-I-N-G."

"I watched you, Rev." Leemaster wipes away the fog his breath has left on the glass. "Watched you and her. Outside, looking in, just like now."

Richard spends a couple of precious seconds thinking about making love to Kinta last night, then turns his thoughts to Christian Martyrs dying in the Coliseum. They look calm in all the paintings. Facing wild animals and wild men with the certain knowledge that God is on their side. Not wondering how they can escape at the last minute. Putting their fate into the invisible hands of their higher power like drug addicts at a NarcAnon meeting.

It's hard for Richard to figure out what he should do when death is standing less than nine feet away. What to say, when it looks like the next few words could be his last.

Something clever that highlights his life like meringue on the top of a lemon pie, or something that makes a murderer put his plans on hold because he wants to hear more.

"I know about you, Oba. Not everything, but some."

The killer comes a step closer. "What do you know, Injun? What does a mud preacher know about a man like me?" He tries to tower over him but they are almost the same size so they stand eye to eye.

Good and evil in a face off. It's clear that Oba Taylor is bad, but how good is Richard Harjo? He's told lies his whole career. He lied to the police yesterday. Framed Burdette Lafleur for murder. Transported class D felony letters to a condemned man. He's stolen from the dead, even though it was an accident. He brought fake holy water to Lorado Mendez, and he's been happy to add adultery to his list—apparently with Anton Leemaster watching.

Fraud, liar, thief, adulterer, are what Richard Harjo calls himself as he reaches into a side pocket and withdraws one of Grandma Angina's tortoise shell hair clips. A few strands of her straight black hair still cling to it. He places the clip into Oba Taylor's hand. Lays it on a black Swastika in his palm. Watches the hand close over it. Reads the letters on Oba's knuckles: "Love." The perfect choice.

"Oh shit." Taylor shrinks a couple of inches as Richard Harjo watches. The inmate stumbles to the cement bunk. Sits down with a thud, as if he'd received advance delivery of the lethal injection promised by the state of Oklahoma. A little taste so he'll be prepared.

"Knowed she was dead," Oba says. "Knowed it without bein' told but now . . . ."

Now he feels it in the palm of his hand.

Anton Leemaster bangs his fists on the viewing window. "Why ain't you doin' nothin', Oba? Nobody will stop you."

But Grandma Angina's spirit has stopped Oba in his tracks. Doused his hatred in the only love the killer had ever known.

"I ain't never killed no one." Oba picks up the Bible Tammy Biggerstaff held while she was in the Waiting Room. Puts the hand on it that doesn't hold a piece of Grandma Angina's soul.

"I ain't no kind of good, but I'm no killer." Swearing he didn't do it the way he swore he did when he thought he didn't care about dying.

"Wolfie Lafleur killed that cop," he said. "I hid his gun underneath my old Airstream Trailer out at the Patch."

"The gun's wiped clean, but Wolfie's prints are on the cartridges," Oba says. "You go find it. See if they ain't."

"Too late to stop the execution," Richard says. "Nine a.m. tomorrow. Everything is set."

"Grandma would want everybody to know I'm innocent. Of murder anyways."

Anton Leemaster pounds on the viewing window. Makes a lot of sounds but none of them are words. Oba Taylor raises the hand he's held on the Waiting Room Bible. Gives Leemaster the finger.

"Fuck you Anton. You ain't no friend to me."

"Me either," Richard says. He gives Anton the finger too. It feels better than filling out a formal complaint no one would take seriously. It feels a lot better than making the sign of the cross.

24

Richard makes no effort to hide the envelope in his back pocket. Oba saw it. The guards have seen it. Nobody asks about it but Holabi Minco.

"Got something for me?" Holabi sits on his cement bunk with his legs crossed Yoga style. No signs of tension in his face. Like a man who has just returned from an extended vacation in Nirvana.

"Heard Leemaster squealin' like a pig on castration day. What did you do to him?" Holabi unfolds his legs and slides them onto the floor. He stands in front of Richard, eye to eye—a very un-Native American thing to do.

"I sort of made friends with Oba Taylor. The guards think I'm a witch for sure." Richard watches Madeline's reflection in the dark centers of Holabi Minco's eyes. Sees her close the door. Watches her through the viewing window as she twists her key in the mechanical lock. Richard sees all these things reflected in Minco's eyes, but he doesn't see himself. As if he's a vampire, whose existence is not acknowledged by light. No matter how he searches, he's not there. How does Holabi do it? Is he doing it?

"They could be right." Minco reaches an arm around Richard and takes the envelope from his back pocket. Pinches part of it between his fingers. Tosses it into his wastebasket, unopened like the last one.

"It's Moving Day," Richard tells him. As if Holabi Minco doesn't know. Now that Oba is in the waiting room. Every H-Unit inmate will move one cell closer to the death chamber.

Richard turns away from Minco, looks at his father's name scratched into the cement wall. How many places did he write it? How many cells in H-Unit?

"Custodial team will search your cell," he tells Holabi. "The guards will go through everything they find. Leemaster . . . ."

"That's when we'll see how much of a witch you really are, Rev. Witches and holy men. Ain't much difference between the two when you get right down to it." He hands Richard three popsicle sticks—all blank.

"Won't be no more calendar sticks for me," he says. "The rest is up to you."

Richard wants to ask what Minco means, but Madeline is at the cell door. She taps on the window, a series of dots and spaces that sounds like an old time prison code. Then she turns the key in the lock and pulls the door open.

"Better come with me Rev. Something's happened."

She tells Holabi, "Everybody's nervous so you'd better step on back."

The extra guards brought in for Oba Taylor are clustered around the door. They form a crescent behind Madeline. She's the one who led Richard to Lorado Mendez's cell, then past the shower room, then to the Waiting Room, where Anton Leemaster went crazy for a little while and had to go out to the employee parking lot for a smoke.

Madeline is the intermediary between witches and prison guards. She's known Holabi Minco since she was a little girl. She's friends with Kinta. She's the one who collects owl feathers from the hallway and talks to the chaplain with the scratches and bruises on his face. She's the one who has to take him back to Lorado Mendez's cell for the second time today.

Holabi Minco slouches against his cell wall as far away from the hallway as he can get. Totally relaxed. Totally relaxed, totally non-threatening, totally in charge of the space around him. "Well, Rev. It looks like you made your bones."

Madeline takes Richard's hand and leads him out of Holabi's cell. The line of guards steps apart and lets them pass. They close ranks again and follow Richard the way they followed Oba Taylor. They want to ask how he got out of the Waiting Room alive. Whose name Richard plans to write on the popsicle sticks they see in his shirt pocket.

They want to ask him how he solved a murder committed years before and never suspected until yesterday. How a preacher could find himself in bed with Kinta Minco doing things Anton Leemaster has been dreaming about for as long as her father had been in prison.

Mostly what they want to ask is why Lorado Mendez died right after Richard's visit.

"Madeline found him," one of the guards says. How could it be otherwise? Madeline has just enough magic to point to a dead man in an H-Unit cell like a needle on a supernatural compass.

The guards know Richard brought a jar of water with him when he visited Lorado Mendez earlier this morning. Class D felony punishable by up to seven years in prison. Seven, like the lucky number at the crap table in the Indian Casinos. Seven, like one of the spiraling sevens around Oba Taylor's eye. The seven deadly sins. The number of days it took God to create the earth. The number of days in a week. The number of colors in a rainbow. A combination of the four sacred directions and the trinity.

"Seven," slips out of Richard Harjo before he can stop it. The guards all take a step back—except for Madeline—because when a man like Richard Harjo talks to himself he might be casting a spell.

"Happened to look in his window," Madeline says. "There he was, lying on the floor." If he'd been in his bunk she wouldn't have thought it strange.

"Fell over while he was on his knees." Madeline points past the crime scene tape someone has strung across the door. "Guess he died while he was praying."

Richard ducks under the tape and nudges the shards of broken Mason jar with his shoe. He nudges Lorado Mendez.

The dead man's head flops over. Water streams out his nose and mouth. Lorado Mendez has drowned himself on Richard's fake Holy Water. A final perfect act of contrition.

Richard's tooth lies beside Lorado Mendez' outstretched hand. Everybody watches the chaplain pick it up. An undeniable link between him and Mendez. Full of DNA that can't be denied if anybody cares to look. Probably no one would, but just in case, Richard swallows the tooth as if it is a piece of communion wafer that's been stopped in the transubstantiation process at the tooth development stage.

The guards watch Richard swallow the tooth, but no one makes a move to stop him. Just like that, Richard Harjo turns tampering with a murder scene into a magic ritual. They won't admit to seeing this to anyone—but they especially won't admit it to Anton Leemaster, who has just returned from smoking Marlboros on the employee parking lot.

"What the fuck happened here?" He wedges himself through the line of guards but stays on the civilian side of the crime scene tape.

"Looks like suicide to me," Richard tells him. "Guess we'd better wait and see what the detectives think."

25

The first thing Richard sees when he steps out of his car is the gibbous moon. The second is the silhouette of a woman standing in the open door of his house.

"Kinta?" The insects in the forest stop their mating calls when Richard says her name. Moonlight doesn't penetrate the shadows that hide her face but the shape in Richard Harjo's doorway could be no one else.

"Kinta." He says her name again to remind himself she's there for him. There for Richard Harjo, who never believed girls like Kinta Minco existed.

"Kinta." He says her name a third time and the insects fill the night with sound again. He doesn't remember walking across the yard, but here he is, kissing her.

"We'd better make it quick." She says this in a whisper so he'll know what it is they have to hurry up and do. She takes one of his hands and places it on her breast in case any doubt remains.

Richard Harjo's hand on a woman's breast before he's said hello. One more thing that's never happened to him before. His list of new and unexpected things is too long to keep track of.

"Anton Leemaster is sure to turn up soon." She takes Richard by the hand that was on her breast and pulls him toward the bedroom. He has to follow, but he does it slowly. He wants to tell her about everything that happened at the prison but she already knows.

"Friends with Oba now. Leemaster freaked out. Lopez killed himself." Kinta summarizes events of the day like a grocery list. She closes the bedroom door behind them. Puts an arm around his waist and pulls him close. Pushes her body into his so she fits against him with no space in between. Heat flows into Richard like a storm front moving up from the Gulf of Mexico.

Women are warmer than men, especially when they are aroused. Richard has heard about things like this. Never believed them until now. So many things he never believed in until now.

They slide toward his double bed like the stylus on a Ouija board, a smooth sweeping motion as if spirits are in charge. They roll onto the bed over the scents and wrinkles of last night's adventures. They fall together, picking up where they left off, as if everything in their lives till now was foreplay.

No one has free will in matters of the heart. Richard has studied things like operant conditioning, and pleasure centers in the brain that respond to chemicals like dopamine and serotonin. According to biologists love can be explained by enzymes and glandular secretions, but Richard Harjo thinks biologists have it wrong. At this moment he thinks science has it wrong about a great many things.

They drop articles of clothing the way snakes shed their skin, exposing bright new sensitive surfaces underneath. Old familiar patterns but with crisp clear lines that have never been touched. Old sensations rediscovered— cleaner and sharper than they will ever be again.

Ideas spark between Richard and Kinta as irresistible as lightning strikes. Perspiration mixes like an elixir that turns their senses into magic receptacles. Richard's breathing and Kinta's find a common rhythm. Fast enough to make them dizzy, not quite fast enough to make them faint. The past falls away like a handful of owl feathers tossed into the air. The future hides inside a cloud so full of rain it erupts into a storm that washes them both away.

Richard doesn't want to look at his watch but he can't stop himself. "Five minutes flat."

"I said we'd have to hurry," Kinta tells him.

Richard's body feels the temperature drop, even though it's August in Oklahoma. His perspiration evaporates as quickly as ethyl alcohol. It makes him shiver, the way Tammy Biggerstaff shivered in the waiting room before Anton Leemaster came to take her away.

"Leemaster." Kinta pulls the name from Richard's mind. It snaps the mood like a stale cracker. She points at the bedroom window at the pair of eyes peering through the small space where the curtains don't come together.

Richard is out of bed before Kinta and good sense can call him back. Out the door, after Anton Leemaster. Doesn't realize he's naked until it's too late to turn back.

The first thing Leemaster sees is the chaplain's testicles. He aims a toe at them but pulls off target because touching that part of Richard's body, even with his shoe seems too much like a homosexual act.

Leemaster wants to look away from Richard's penis, but it pulls at his attention like an elastic chord.

Richard swings a roundhouse punch. Sure to make contact, because Leemaster is not accustomed the presence of an aggressive naked man unless he's supervising a death row shower in H-Unit.

All the energy absorbed from Kinta Minco is concentrated in Richard's fist as it follows a perfect arc and collides with Anton Leemaster's temple.

The guard's features distort with the blow. A mist of blood sprays out his nose and hangs in the air like a swarm of microscopic gnats. Leemaster stumbles sideways. Slips to the ground, his eyes still locked on Richard's penis.

He crawls backward while the Chaplain massages his hand. Too disoriented to find his balance. Too much double vision from the blow: Two naked Richard Harjos with two penises, massaging two fists doubling up to take another swing.

But Leemaster has a pistol.

It takes a while for an angry naked man to notice things like deadly weapons, but now Richard sees it clearly. Its square shape. A black hole in the end of the barrel like the eye of a great white shark, trying to decide if he's worth the trouble.

The muzzle of Anton Leemaster's pistol swings back and forth, as the guard tries to decide which of the double images is real and which is phantom.

"Two souls." Richard proves to Anton Leemaster he understands the problem.

"One goes to the Happy place and one stays to haunt the killer."

Anton Leemaster fires his pistol. One muzzle flash. Neither Richard falls to the ground because the shooter never chose. His bullet passes between the pair of witch spirits and flies into the forest. He doesn't shoot again because Kinta Minco has come outside.

She and Richard watch Anton back away, moving like a bird with a broken wing until he reaches the woods that border Richard's property.

"He lost his shoe." Kinta points to the spit polished DOC uniform shoe that is reflecting the final light of the setting sun.

"I'll take it to him tomorrow," Richard tells her.

Kinta takes the hand that struck Leemaster and kisses it. "Want to go inside? I don't think he'll be coming back."

26

The forest fills with moonlight, and Wolfie knows the ecstasy is kicking in. *Rolling with Molly.* The phase circles his mind like an audio loop. Molly. E's little sister. Pure as the Virgin Mary. Gentle. Safe.

Wolfie knows that's bullshit. Molecules are molecules. Dope is dope, no matter where you buy it or what the seller promises. His jaws lock together like a pit bull's, but that doesn't stop him from grinding his teeth. He listens to the crunch of enamel turning into sand. It sounds like love.

His poison ivy itches more than ever, but now the itch belongs to someone else. Someone who lives outside the E-dimension. He'll quit using when the time is right. Give it up cold turkey without a clinic, or a doctor, or a twelve-step program. But the time is definitely not right.

Not until Kinta understands she's stained his soul with mud and there's no going back.

An image of her takes shape on his left shoulder. Too close to see with his eyes, but he knows it's there. Like a hologram of Princess Leah saying "Help me, Obi Wan Kenobi. You're my only hope."

He whispers, "Help is on the way," and listens for an answer.

Nothing but cicadas, and owls, and leaves stirring in the Oklahoma wind, so he keeps moving. The force guides Wolfie the way it guided Luke Skywalker before he realized Leah was his sister. Not a stepsister like Tammy. A real one.

His thoughts are hijacked by a shrill howling noise. A coyote calling to the moon? He listens for almost a minute before he realizes it's his voice. Even then he can't stop, but he can shift into the silent mode, so only the evil mud spirits living in his head can hear the sound.

He's almost forgotten why he's in the woods. That's the way it goes when he's on ecstasy. The dose is almost always not enough or too much. Almost impossible to find the *just right* dose.

Molly is the Goldilocks of recreational drugs.

Wolfie knows the exact moment when he reaches his peak. The gibbous moon switches on like a million-watt bulb. It fills his eyes with light that bounced off the moon 1.3 seconds before it falls through his Molly-dilated pupils. A perfect bank shot from the sun. He learned all about the speed of light on NOVA. And the special and general theories of relativity, and the big bang theory.

Science is very interesting to Wolfie Lafleur, even the Theory of Evolution, which everybody knows was invented by an English Jew to trick white people into thinking their grandparents are monkeys.

Wolfie feels like the biggest, most important monkey in the world as he walks among the cedars and post oak trees, ignoring the burning poison-ivy itch on the lower half of his body. He's the smartest, most dangerous animal in the forest, on a hunt for . . . .

He sorts through his memory for few seconds before, "Kinta," comes out of his mouth in another coyote howl.

Her name bounces off the trees and comes back to him, and everything makes sense. Wolfie Lafleur is exactly where he's supposed to be every hour of every day and right now he's in the woods that edges up against a prison chaplain's yard. Kinta's boyfriend.

He's almost forgotten the pistol in his hand, but it suddenly feels heavy. And slick. Slick as a bar of soap in a prison shower. His palms are lubricated with ecstasy sweat. The drug seeps through his pores, saturates his clothing. His temperature is 105° at least. Hot enough to catch the world on fire. One Wolfie touch will kill a man, and he's ready to kill every man in the world if that's what it takes to be next in line for Kinta. The murder starts with Richard Harjo.

Cut grass around the preacher's house butts up against the forest in a line so sharp and clean it might have been drawn with a straight edge and a Sharpie.

A brown-skinned naked man is fighting with a white man in the yard. Kinta is inside the house. Behind a window, watching everything that is happening because of her.

What other reason can there be? Everything happens because of Kinta Minco. Free will is an illusion for every man who's fallen under her spell.

The naked one is Richard Harjo. The preacher's enemy is the guard who passed out popsicles on the day the state of Oklahoma killed Tammy.

"Floating man." Wolfie repeats the last two words his stepsister said before she died. His tongue remembers the taste of orange ice as he prepares to put a bullet into the back of the preacher who held Tammy's hand when the time came.

He closes one eye and lines up the groove in the rear sight of the pistol with the center of the chaplain's back. He shifts the barrel until the front sight floats over Richard Harjo's spinal cord. Careful, because Kinta Minco is coming out of the house and the bullet isn't meant for her.

Wolfie tries to draw a deep breath, but his lungs are already full. He holds the pistol in a double-handed grip to control the Molly-tremors.

The white man on the ground has a pistol too, but he can't make up his mind where to point it.

Perfect timing. Wolfie will pull the trigger so that his gunshot noise overlaps with the guard's. Kinta will never know Wolfie Lafleur killed her boyfriend.

But before he can send the message to his trigger finger a flash fills his ecstasy-dilated eyes. An explosion starts his ears ringing like a supernatural alarm clock. A lightning bolt slaps him in the face at the exact moment he is supposed to pull the trigger—but can't.

Wolfie staggers backward into the forest. His mouth tastes like blood. His head throbs in perfect time with his heartbeat, which is following a muddy, syncopated, reggae rhythm.

This is what it feels like to be shot by a stupid bungling prison guard.

Molly turns the pain in Wolfie's head into energy. The energy supercharges his need for revenge, but the target of that revenge has changed.

He doesn't know how long he's been running through the forest, but he's on the trail of the man who shot him. Richard Harjo isn't important anymore.

"Anton Leemaster." He remembers how the name sounded when his father read it from the guard's ID tag. Remembers how the Anton Leemaster smiled when Tammy died.

Blood from Wolfie's head wound has matted his hair like a gigantic dab of Brylcreem. The skin puckers around the furrow of raw tissue on his scalp.

"Flesh wound," he tells himself, even though there's not much flesh on a man's head. There's probably some bone involved, but he'll worry about that after he's killed Anton Leemaster.

The guard looks at Wolfie over his shoulder. The moonlight illuminates his fear. Wolfie sees the hint of recognition in Leemaster's eyes. There was no blood on Wolfie's face when he watched his stepsister die.

Leemaster and Wolfie remember the guard's pistol at the same time.

Wolfie's right hand feels a lot lighter than it did when he was planning to kill Richard Harjo. It floats up into gunfight position but it is empty. The guard's hand is filled with a semi automatic pistol.

"Shit." What else is there for a Molly-addled murderer to say when it's clear things aren't going to work out.

"Who the hell are you?" Leemaster wants to know before he pulls the trigger.

"Wolfie Lafleur." It's the only bit of information Wolfie knows for sure. His name is thick and sticky because his saliva has gone the way of his pistol.

He tries again, "Wolfie Lafleur." Better this time. His heart rate slows to the aerobic level. The moonlight dims so that Anton Leemaster's face looks like a camp counselor's who is entertaining elementary school kids with ghost stories.

"What do you want?" Leemaster asks.

Fair question, so Wolfie tells him. "To kill you."

He realizes at that moment he's been holding his breath ever since he stopped running and now he's used up all his air.

"Oxygen debt," Wolfie says. Something he learned on the Discovery Channel that he's sure Leemaster will want to know.

"Crazy bastard," Anton Leemaster fires his pistol just as Wolfie faints.

Wolfie Lafleur is pretty sure he isn't dead because you never hear the one that gets you, and his ears are ringing louder than ever.

"Stop scratching. You'll make that poison ivy spread." Kinta Minco's voice. Wolfie would know it anywhere. He opens his eyes and there she is, saving his life exactly like she did before.

"Drink this." She's propped his head on a stone like Jacob's pillow in one of the bible verses Burdette used to read to him.

"It's chamomile and thyme for the itching," she says. "Lavender to relax and a touch of clover to clear your head."

A beam of sunlight breaks through the forest canopy and illuminates Kinta. Acknowledges her as a goddess.

He wants to kiss her, but his mouth is full of tea.

Kinta tips his head back and rubs his throat, the way she would make a stubborn cat swallow a pill. There's too much tea in Wolfie's mouth, but he takes it in a single painful gulp. His esophagus aches until it spills the liquid into his stomach.

"I love you," he tells her. "More than the guard. More than the preacher. More than anybody."

She tips the cup of tea into his mouth again. He swallows it a little at a time. It leaves a confusing sensation in his throat like hot and cold changing places so quickly he can't keep track.

"Cannabis flowers," Kinta tells him. "From the farm near the Patch."

She knows what he's thinking so he doesn't have to say anything more.

"Richard's gone to help Oba Taylor die." She forces another swallow of tea into his mouth. The liquid is thick and sweet near the bottom of the cup, with a hint of bitterness hiding behind the sugars.

"He'll help my father next." She tells him.

"Night of the lunar eclipse." She forces another sip of tea. "One way or another, it will be over for my dad on the last day of Women's Month."

Wolfie wants to tell Kinta he loves her one more time, but his mouth is full of leaves and stems and something slimy and bitter like —

"Mushrooms." Kinta pulls Wolfie to his feet. She points him toward the sun and gives him a little push.

Like every man who has ever been in love, Wolfie Lafleur follows the path of least resistance. The last time Kinta pushed him he wound up in the Patch. He wonders if he's headed there again.

27

Anton Leemaster stands in the employee parking lot surrounded by crushed Marlboro butts. His hands are the color of nicotine. His face is the color of soured milk except for the purple bruise that shades his left cheek like a partial eclipse.

He jumps when Richard drops his uniform shoe onto the pile of cigarette butts.

"Brown shoes aren't regulation." Richard Harjo points to the scuffed slip-on loafers Leemaster is wearing today. He sounds official, like a man who got the better of a spying guard and wants to make the most of it.

Leemaster recoils from the chaplain's voice. Raises his arms in a not-quite-defensive pugilistic posture. Stutters when he starts to talk but gets control of his voice long enough to deliver an apology that is right on the edge of sincerity.

"K-kind of lost it, Rev. Shouldn't have spied on you. It's the girl. You know how things are." He starts to bend over and pick up his shoe but changes his mind because Richard Harjo is close enough to kick him.

Guards don't carry pistols in the prison. They aren't allowed to keep pistols in their cars either, while they are on DOC property, but Richard is pretty certain he'd find one in Leemaster's automobile if he knew where it was parked.

He points at the shoe and steps back far enough so the guard can snatch it up and slink away to the prison entrance. Like a dog stealing a pork chop from the dinner table.

Leemaster stops inside the door and stares at Richard Harjo. If looks could kill, the chaplain would be as lifeless as the used Marlboro butts at his feet.

Last week Richard would have been intimidated by the guard. Last week he would have considered filing a complaint that would make its way through disciplinary committees for months until someone high up in administration took responsibility for ignoring it. Leemaster would have things to say in his own defense if it came to that. Things about the chaplain bringing contraband to death row inmates and sleeping with a condemned killer's daughter.

Richard takes a step toward Leemaster and the guard disappears into the prison's interior.

"I'll catch you later," Richard Harjo calls after him. "In the execution chamber." Where Leemaster will help strap Oba Taylor to the gurney and Richard will try to make his dying easier.

Oba Taylor stands as Madeline opens the Waiting Room Door and allows Richard Harjo to go inside.

"What time is it, Rev?" Taylor's eyes are angry. He's holding Grandma Angina's hair clip in one hand and a pair of panties smeared with steak sauce in the other.

Tammy Biggerstaff's?

"Don't think so," Taylor answers the question Richard didn't ask out loud. What else could a chaplain have on his mind when he sees a pair of cotton DOC women's underwear in a murderer's hand?

"Man's got to hang on to something, don't he, Rev?"

"Eight thirty," Richard tells him. One question out of phase already. He reaches into his pocket and find's Grandma Angina's second hair clip. Holds it out to Oba Taylor, closest to the hand that's holding the cotton panties. Makes him choose which one he wants in his last half hour of life.

Oba tries to take the hair clip without dropping the undergarment, but Richard pulls it back. "Grandma wouldn't want her property to keep that kind of company," he says.

Oba looks like he might object, but he tosses the cotton underwear into his wastebasket. "Let the custodians have their fun, I guess." He takes the hair clip. One in each hand. The tension in his shoulders flows into the clips and vanishes like electricity that's found a shortcut to the ground.

"Grandma's is better than a whore, anyway. Right, Rev?"

There's no good answer to that question so Richard looks at his watch again. "Eight thirty-two." Wishes he hadn't told Oba Taylor how fast his time is evaporating. "Want to pray?"

Taylor looks at the hair clips and says, "I think it might be too late to help." He walks to the door of the Waiting Room and looks through the viewing window into the hallway.

"You been to the Patch, Rev. You seen how things are." He angles his head so he can look down the hallway toward the security station. "The Hooded Men will walk this way, won't they, Rev?"

Oba Taylor kisses Grandma's hair clips one at a time. Touches each of them with the tip of his tongue. "Got to pass by. Ain't no other way to the chamber. What time is it getting to be?"

Richard looks at his watch again. Two more minutes have raced by, as if time is being distorted by the gravitational pull of a black hole inside the execution chamber four feet away.

"Ah." Oba Taylor has found what he's looking for. "There they are." He steps away from the cell door so Richard can see the three executioners walking side by side. They stop in front of the Waiting Room and look inside at Oba Taylor. One of them waves. Taylor waves back and smiles.

Then they walk away.

"One of them has a limp, Rev." Oba says. "You see the one with the limp?"

He looks at Richard's watch. Tracks the second hand as it makes another circuit.

"Time moves in circles, Rev. Like horses running around a track. Finish line is where you started out." He kisses Grandma Angina's hair clips as the second hand passes the number three, and six, and nine, and twelve, creating fifteen-second rituals.

Oba Taylor winks at Richard with the eye at the center of the spiraling sevens. As if the two men know each other better than they do. As if they share a secret.

"You been to the Patch. You seen how I came up. What would you pray for if you was me?" Taylor walks over to his bunk. He picks up the Waiting Room Bible. Reads aloud from the Book of Revelation. Stumbles over thees, and thous, and whosoevers.

"This crap don't make no sense, Rev. Think you can tell me what it means?"

Richard looks at this watch again. "Eight forty-one." As if that explains everything Oba Taylor needs to know.

Oba doesn't resist when Madeline opens the door and four jittery guards come in with their shock sticks. Anton Leemaster follows them in carrying shackles.

"It ain't a long walk, Oba, but we're afraid to let you make the trip unrestrained."

"A lot can happen in four paces." Oba clenches his fists around Grandma's hair clips and holds his hands out for the cuffs.

"You look like shit, Anton." He stands at attention and flexes the muscles in his jaw as Anton Leemaster fastens the shackles around his ankles. The chains don't look substantial enough to hold the prisoner, but this is the way it's always done.

Leemaster tugs on the chains. Assures himself they are secure. He steps on Oba Taylor's foot—shod in paper slippers since they moved him to the Waiting Room. No reaction from the prisoner. Richard sees that Leemaster is wearing his uniform shoes again. Cruel shoes for a cruel man. Shoes that step on the few rights and the little dignity a condemned man has in his last minutes.

"What time is it now, Rev?" Oba Taylor asks.

"Eight fifty," Richard tells him. "Still time for a prayer if you want it."

"Hell no, Rev. Let's go on and do this thing."

28

The prisoner is peaceful on the four-foot walk to the chamber. He takes short deliberate steps like a bride moving down the aisle toward the biggest turning point in her life. The chain between his ankles is loose because security is tight. Oba Taylor's stride is slow and flat-footed, but there is no way to make the walk last more than four seconds.

The door to the execution chamber is bright yellow, like the door to the Waiting Room, but it has no pass-through, no conversation vents, and no viewing window—a featureless yellow portal to the last room the condemned man will ever enter. Oba Taylor hums a few bars of "Yellow Submarine" while Anton Leemaster fumbles with the latch. The drug-oriented Beatles song is transformed into a funeral dirge.

Richard wonders if the color scheme is repeated in other death rows, in other states, in other countries. What theories of interior design hold sway in prisons? Yellow is nature's warning color. Yellow jackets, bees, poison frogs, coral snakes, Gila monsters. A bright, easily identifiable color that broadcasts danger to everyone who cares to look. Easy to see. Easy to avoid, but there is no way for Oba Taylor to avoid the death chamber. He pauses in the open door, as if this is the place he's chosen to make his stand.

Leemaster touches him with the business end of a shock stick. No juice, but the feel of the electrodes is enough to get him moving. He walks past the witness room door, which is steel reinforced and double locked but the inmate can't know that.

"Madeline's got the popsicle concession today," Anton Leemaster says. As if that's something Oba Taylor needs to know.

"Hot as a bitch kitten in the witness room," the guard tells him. "No ventilation at all." He nudges Oba with the shock stick again. "Witnesses have been cookin' in there since seven."

Oba doesn't know who's come to watch him die. Condemned men have no access to the witness list. The viewing window of his cell is covered when the interested parties walk by so his ghost won't be able to hold a grudge.

He rattles his shackles so the witnesses will know the show's about to start. "That's the sound of a dead man walkin', in case anybody's interested."

The short hallway is wide enough to accommodate a gurney so Oba Taylor's body can be rolled away after he's been killed and wrapped in plastic like a cheap cut of meat marked down for quick sale. Oba's remains will be held in the execution room until the State Medical Examiner confirms he's dead, and the technician removes the eighteen gauge needle from his arm, and the witnesses finish their popsicles and the Hooded Men walk down the H-Unit hallway in full view of the other condemned prisoners waiting their turns on the table.

The dead man in the body bag will be wheeled out after the lights inside the death row cells have been turned off. The Pittsburgh County morgue wagon will meet the guards in the employee parking lot where Anton Leemaster smokes his cigarettes and imagines how it would feel to place his hand on Kinta Minco's breasts.

Richard Harjo usually leads the parade to the death chamber on execution day. He usually walks beside the condemned inmate, mumbling prayers that sound like magic incantations. Bargaining with God, as if the afterlife were a leather jacket on sale in Tijuana.

Not today. Not when the killer is Oba Taylor who is as scary as a rabid pit bull. Today Richard walks into the chamber behind the special detail of prison guards who'll spring into action if Oba loses it at the last minute like everybody thinks he will.

The Hooded Men are already in their cubicle, waiting for the warden's signal to push their buttons and share responsibility for the execution. The warden stands beside the curtained witness room window by the telephone that has never rung in the history of Oklahoma. The technician waits with his IV tubing and his needles, dressed in green scrubs with bleach splotches on the knees.

"The Fuck . . . ." Oba is the first inmate to ever use that word this close to death. Condemned inmates usually turn meek and quiet in their final minutes, just in case there really is a supernatural parole officer watching from his witness room in the sky.

"This ain't happening . . . ." Oba sounds angry and reasonable at the same time, like a speeder arguing with a cop. "No way this is right."

Richard considers making a run for it. Back down the short hallway, to the yellow execution room door that is already shut and locked behind him, but he steps into the death chamber instead.

"What's the trouble?" Richard asks. There's so much trouble in this little room where a man is going to die in time to make the ten o'clock news. Anton Leemaster is already unshackling Oba even though the inmate's temper is coming to a boil.

Oba's fists are clenched around Grandma Angina's hair clips but his eyes are locked on the African American technician who is smiling back at him—ninety percent fear, ten percent amicability. The technician makes gestures with his arms that look like a mix of religious supplication and charades.

Leemaster says, "Calm down, Oba. We're on a tight schedule here." He starts to wind the shackles into a neat bundle but drops them on the floor instead, because it looks like he's going to need both hands—and the shock stick—to control Oba now that he's unchained.

"A colored man?" Oba Taylor's way of being polite. "A goddamned colored man's gonna put the killing needle in my arm?"

"Sorry, man, if I didn't do it somebody else would," the technician tells him.

Richard wonders if they learn that line in execution school.

The tech hides the needle behind his back, pretends he's an innocent bystander who just happens to be inside the death chamber at the wrong moment. His face glistens with perspiration. Wet circles spread under his arms like oil slicks. He drops his needle and his tubing onto the death chamber floor and edges toward the warden.

Oba holds his arms straight out like a Nazi mime transforming crucifixion into performance art. Anton Leemaster grabs one arm. A second guard takes the other. Both of them together aren't as strong as Oba Taylor.

The remaining three guards huddle behind Richard Harjo, realizing for the first time they are in a small room with a very dangerous man who has nothing to lose.

Leemaster and his brother guard know they need to use their shock sticks but Oba Taylor's muscles are pumped full of rage and the prison guards don't dare let go.

"Little help!" The warden says, as if order can be restored by a show of leadership.

The guards behind Richard Harjo pretend there's no way for them to get into the action.

"Preacher's in the way," one of them tells Leemaster.

Richard Harjo feels very much in the way. He feels very much an obstacle between Oba Taylor and the objects of his hatred. He should call for peace and calm, but those words seem to have lost their force, so he cries, "Help!" instead.

Oba Taylor puts a stop to the conversation in the death chamber with a Rebel yell. When he has everybody's attention he says, "Wolfie Lafleur murdered that Jew cop. I ain't killed nobody—yet."

"Proof is at the Patch," he says. "The preacher knows."

The Three Hooded Men step out of their cubicle where three unmarked buttons are mounted on the wall, dividing guilt into thirds. The hooded figures step toward Oba Taylor as if they mean to do more than push buttons. One of them has a belt in his hand. A wide leather belt with the name OTTO hand tooled on the back. Easy to read because it says the same thing forward and backward. What it means is this man comes from the Patch.

The hooded man says, "Hold it there, partner," and swings his belt across Anton Leemaster's face.

The three hooded men attack the guards with a fury that more than compensates for their small numbers.

Leemaster steps away from Oba. Presses his hands over the mark left by Otto's name belt. Letters show between his fingers—a crisp clear palindrome label assigning credit for the injury.

Oba Taylor turns his full attention to the remaining guard who looks like he's attempting a chin up on the inmate's outstretched arm. Taylor lifts the guard and throws him at the witness window.

The guard smashes into the safety glass, leaves a body-shaped spider web impression, and drops to the floor beside the warden. He curls into a tight round ball, like a fetus hiding from an abortionist's curette.

Oba snatches up another guard, and tosses him. Identical ballistics. This one makes it through the safety glass as the curtains snap open.

The witnesses have lost their taste for death now that it's uncertain who it is who's going to die. They scramble for the door, which has been double locked for their safety until the execution is finished.

The three hooded men turn their attention to the warden, who is trying desperately to look like he's got everything under control while he calls for help with the death chamber telephone.

"There's no way out of here." The warden looks at Oba Taylor—tries to reason with a man who has swastikas and spiraling sevens and Christian Identity Movement numerology on his face. Tries to calm Oba Taylor down. Convince him to lie down on the execution gurney and accept his needle like a man.

"It's the law, Taylor." The warden looks to Richard Harjo for support but Richard is watching the interested parties in the witness room crowd through the exit.

"Tell him, Rev," the warden says. "He's only making things worse."

While Richard considers how things could be worse for Oba Taylor, Anton Leemaster shakes off the trauma of his belt whipping. He picks up his shock stick and sneaks underneath the killing gurney while the Hooded Men fight off the other guards.

Oba Taylor screams as Leemaster touches his shock stick to the number eighty-eight on his forehead.

"Heil Hitler asshole." Leemaster stands beside Oba, waiting for the convulsions to stop, and when they do, he touches the electrodes to Oba's chest and empties the charge into the inmate's heart.

The Hooded Men's motivation ends with Oba Taylor's dying breath.

The inmate's hands fall open and release Grandma Angina's hair clips onto the execution chamber floor. The Hooded Men all look at Richard Harjo.

Otto drops his belt. "Oba's with Grandma now," he says. "I guess that's a better place."

The death chamber door opens and six members of the prison emergency response team crowd in. Their grim faces are distorted behind their helmets and their Plexiglas shields. They are an impenetrable wall, ready to strike at the first sign of resistance.

The Hooded Men drop back.

Richard watches Madeline through the shattered witness room window. The room is empty except for the female guard. Her lips and teeth are stained the color of the popsicles melting in the witness chairs.

Double stick strawberry day.

The African American technician takes Oba's pulse and talks to someone on his headset. "This motherfucker's dead," he says. "Not a regular execution. I'll still get paid. Right?"

One of the Hooded Men limps over to Oba. He pulls off his hood and robe, struggles to hold his pants up—now that his belt is gone—but they slip to his knees the way Burdette Lafleur's pants slid down after Kinta stabbed him. He turns his back to the emergency response team and clasps his hands behind him, ready for the handcuffs.

"Be different if I had my shotgun." Otto's boxer shorts are laundered and free of holes. Probably set out by his mother, Richard guesses, when she sent him off to break Oba Taylor out of prison. There are things all mothers have in common. Even mothers from the Patch.

29

There's no way to rush out of a maximum-security prison. Every hallway intersection is a small interior room with bulletproof glass walls and sliding doors. Guards behind one glass wall check identities against lists on computer screens before they decide which doors will slide open and which will remain closed. There are fourteen such intersections between H-Unit and the parking lot where Richard Harjo means to go as soon as he passes his final inspection.

He watches Kinta through the bulletproof glass of the fourteenth set of doors as she steps out of the woods behind the lot. He waves to her, even though he knows it's impossible to see into the prison interior from more than a few feet away.

She waves back. Is it a sense of timing? Some kind of witchy clairvoyance? Two weeks ago Richard would have said no such thing exists, but now that he's met Holabi Minco and slept with Minco's daughter . . . .

The guards glance at Richard but they don't make eye contact. They pass him through exactly the way he was passed through every security bottleneck that leads from H-Unit to the outside world. None of the guards wants to talk to a man who was in the death chamber where Oba Taylor died when but definitely not how he was supposed to. Richard wonders if these are the same guards who allowed Oba's relatives to walk into the prison disguised as his executioners.

He doesn't blame them, but he's certain someone will.

The final door is made of untinted glass so employees can see what they are getting into when they are coming and going. The sliding doors have heavy steel frames. They roll on bearings, pulled by electric motors strong enough to move a locomotive. They are wide enough for prison officials to ride through in golf carts. Wide enough for two guards to walk beside a gurney with Oba Taylor's body on it. That will happen later on today, after homicide detectives decide electrocuting a condemned killer in the execution chamber of a state penitentiary is not a crime.

Kinta throws her arms around Richard as soon as he passes through the exit. "Radio says Oba Taylor's dead. Big fight in the execution chamber." She takes his hand and leads him across the parking lot.

"His family," Kinta says. "Couldn't let the state kill Oba without trying, could they?" As her fingers lace through Richard's, he feels the tension in his shoulders drain away. Each step he takes is lighter than the one before, as if Kinta Minco is a helium balloon lifting him high above his prison troubles.

The world looks better as they move away from the entrance. The air carries the scent of pine and wildflowers. Birds call to each other from blackjack and cedar trees. The afternoon sun turns the bullet holes in Richard's windshield into circular rainbows. Everything in front of Richard is peaceful and beautiful while Kinta holds his hand. The world behind him is dark and ill-defined, like the memory of a nightmare unraveling in the morning light.

"The Hooded Men . . . ." Richard wants to tell Kinta what happened, but can't quite find a starting point.

"Otto Taylor," she says.

He doesn't expect her to know about Otto from the Patch, but apparently she knows everything. Kinta puts her arms around him again. Kisses him even though the security guard is watching from the gate. Up close she smells like flower-scented shampoo and pheromones and bacon.

Richard wants to ask her about the bacon smell but she covers his mouth with hers. When the kiss is finished she traces the contours of his lips with the tip of her tongue—sloppy and charming, like a five-year-old trying to keep her colors inside the lines. It's hard to ask about bacon with so much going on. The wet circle on Richard's lips tingles as Kinta pulls back. She locks eyes with his for a moment. Moves away but only a few inches, as if she's struggling against a powerful magnetic field.

Animal magnetism. Richard has been drawn to women before. Mostly they haven't been drawn to him, but even when they were it was nothing like this. Her smile stirs memories of things that went through his mind last night, right before his spirit combined with hers to form a mixture as smooth as sipping whiskey and as explosive as nitroglycerine.

Spirits. Another thing he didn't believe in until he met Kinta Minco. He wants to say something to her. Something important that will make it possible to get a grip on his emotions.

What he says is, "Dopamine." The neurochemical responsible for addiction, love and infatuation. He learned about the biochemistry of love while he studied for his PhD. Things don't feel that simple to Richard Harjo anymore. Not as simple as hormones. Not as simple as religion either. The bond between him and Kinta is well beyond one-word explanations. It's strong and warm and has something—but not everything—to do with sex.

His eyes explore the contours of her body. She's wearing jeans and a T-shirt with words across the chest advertising Geraldine's Chicken Fried Steak. He sees through the clothing as if he had X-ray vision. His hands want to explore what his eyes see and his brain imagines—maybe because of dopamine, or because of something no biochemist ever imagined. A tremor starts in his fingers, spreads up his arms, and starts his body trembling.

Love or epilepsy?

"Don't overthink it, Richard." Kinta opens the driver's door. Scoots behind the steering wheel. Holds her hand out. Wiggles her fingers until Richard gives her the keys.

"Are we going to the Patch?" he asks.

She engages the ignition and holds it until the starter motor screams.

"Oba's last wish," Richard answers his own question. "What else can we do?"

"How witchy do you feel?" Kinta waves to the guard as they drive through the gate. She adjusts the rearview mirror. Adjusts the side view mirror.

"Anton Leemaster isn't following us yet," she says. "He will, you know. It won't take him long to find the Patch."

"It always comes to violence in the end. You know that, don't you, Richard?"

He watches the prison get smaller as Kinta drives toward Indian Nations Turnpike. It shrinks as they move away, until he can't see it anymore.

"No Anton," Richard says. "At least not yet." He studies Kinta in profile. Watches the wind blow her Native American hair into flourishes around her face.

"Why do you think he's coming?" Richard reaches over and pinches a lock of hair between a thumb and finger. It leaves a sheen of Kinta-oil on his fingerprints when he lets go. "Because his name was written on a popsicle stick?"

"Because he has a map," Kinta tells him. "Two maps, just in case. You brought them to my dad's cell yourself."

Richard doesn't feel very witchy at all when he hears this. Bewitched is how he feels. He sniffs the oil on his fingers. Flower shampoo and pheromones. No bacon scent at all.

30

There is an empty car parked at the rest stop on Indian Nations Turnpike where the secret road to the Patch begins. It doesn't belong to Anton Leemaster. Kinta backs into a parking place. The way policemen and bank robbers park their cars so they can leave quickly when the time comes.

She turns the engine off but leaves the key in the ignition. She settles back and watches the restroom. "Want to make sure it's not an ambush."

Words like ambush make Richard nervous. He used to own a pistol. Doesn't any more. Didn't like the way it bucked in his hand. Didn't like the way tiny hot flecks of gunpowder residue stung his skin. Didn't like the way he smelled after he'd wasted a dozen shots trying to hit the target. A man who shoots as poorly as Richard Harjo is probably better off bringing prayers to a gunfight, but still . . . .

An overweight blonde woman leads a small boy out of the women's restroom and gets into her car. She looks at the bullet holes in Richard's windshield while she fastens her son into his car seat.

Richard stares back. Can't get the word ambush out of his mind, even though it's clear this woman and her child have nothing to do with Oba Taylor, or Anton Leemaster, or the Patch.

Kinta takes his head in both her hands. Kisses him on the lips hard enough to make his old bruises throb.

When she stops, Richard looks at the overweight mother and her child again. She's no longer looking at his car. No longer wondering about the bullet holes in his windshield. She's disgusted rather than curious. Ready to drive away and try to get the picture of the trashy people in the trashy car out of her mind. Hoping her little boy won't ask about the wrestling match he might have seen.

"The essence of deception," Kinta tells him. "Make witnesses want to look somewhere else."

"We walk from here." She pulls the keys from the ignition. Places them in Richard's hand. "You never answered my question. How witchy do you feel?"

"Pretty witchy, I guess." He looks across the dry creek at the two stones that mark to the road to Grandma's place. "But I kind of wish I had a gun."

"No point in trying to hide," Kinta says. "Drug and whiskey people have dogs. Oba Taylor's people have paranoia. Impossible to sneak in here without being seen."

"The Patch." Richard likes the sound of the secret town on the other side of a dried up stream.

"It's an open secret," Kinta says. "A place where low-class criminals put their differences aside." Skinheads, meth cooks, pot smokers, juicers and plain old disagreeable assholes live together in peace and harmony.

"Like a John Lennon song," Richard says, "With a Country and Western backup band."

John Lennon never sang about pit bulls. Kinta and Richard haven't made it past the first skull-and-crossbones sign when three of them run out of the underbrush making sounds like an orange caught in a garbage disposal.

Richard's first impulse is to run, but his second is to protect Kinta. He steps in front of her, clenches his fists, ready to kick and shout and sound like he's the kind of man who faces down killer dogs every day.

No people appear with rifles, at least not yet. That's either a good sign, or a sign the meth dealers have total confidence in their canine defense.

Two of the dogs have brindle coats. One is solid black. Their faces contort into pit bull smiles that look sweet and deadly at the same time. The animals give off *Nothing Personal* vibes. Just doing our jobs. Their tails wag as they pick up speed. No hint of rage but they look as compact and indestructible as torpedoes as they race through the sparse grass toward their targets.

Richard considers picking up a rock, but there is so little time before the dogs will be on them. He wants to take a step in their direction. Show them he's not afraid—even though he is. He manages to lift a foot, but it won't go any further so he puts it down again.

He's heard animals can smell fear. Wonders if he can smell it too, because right now the air around Richard Harjo is saturated with his fear, and it smells a lot like bacon.

The dogs spread out as they approach Kinta and Richard. They put their noses down. Their tongues lap against the ground. They make grunting happy noises, still like garbage disposals but not so threatening anymore.

Kinta stands beside Richard. One hand holds a plastic bag. The other reaches inside and tosses bits of bacon to the three dogs that were going to eat them a moment ago but now are their best friends.

"Here," she offers Richard the bag. "Meth cooks never remember to feed their watch dogs."

The animals lap strips of bacon from Richard's hands. They lick the grease off of his fingers. By the time they get all the way to his naked skin they are fast friends. Kinta goes down on her knees and pets the dogs. Finds a spot on each of them that makes them tremble. Tames them the way she tamed Richard Harjo.

The pit bulls take turns sneezing.

"Their way of welcoming you to the pack," Kinta says.

The animals don't require a response from Richard Harjo. They accept him as soon as it's clear that's what Kinta wants.

"Witches need to plan ahead," she tells him. "The more plans the better." She stands and walks toward the Taylor section of the patch. The dogs follow, in hopes of getting another treat. Richard follows too, for pretty much the same reason.

31

Richard is sure they are being watched, even though he sees no one. A flash of movement in a marijuana field, a noise among the cedar trees.

He's sure the people watching them have guns. Doesn't practically everyone in Oklahoma? They aren't shooting because they've never seen anything like this before: a man walking with a pretty girl leading an entourage of pit bulls into the Taylor compound. Strangers usually drive into the Patch if they have business. Sometimes they drive back with shot out rear windows. Sometimes they don't drive back at all.

Kinta puts an arm around his waist and bumps him with her hip. "Look natural," she tells him, as if that's possible.

The sexual tension pulls at Richard like wet rawhide that's been put in the sun. So close their steps are synchronized. So close their bodies sway in identical harmonic motions. His hand slides down Kinta's back until it comes to rest at the top of her buttocks. He starts to take it further, but one of the pit bulls gooses him with its nose. Richard is surprised to find a dog nose is more effective at taking his mind off sex than gunmen in the forest. Still, it doesn't work a hundred percent.

"Plenty of time for all that later," Kinta says. Her mind on business, the way only a woman's mind can be.

Richard sees another flash of light in a copse of trees that borders the Taylor compound. Not a muzzle flash because there's no noise, no pain, no blood, no unsatisfying life passing before his eyes. The clearing around Grandma's house is exactly as he remembers except there is no dark skinned man in a cowboy hat telling him to "Hold on there, partner." Otto is in custody at the prison along with two other close relations of Oba Taylor because Oba was Grandma's favorite.

"Nobody's home." Richard looks at the Taylor family house, that's crawled across the yard over the last century leaving rotting timbers and collapsing walls behind, pushing ahead with cheap new construction. Plywood is staked and propped for a cement slab beside the aluminum sided frame house where Grandma Angina was laid out for a final viewing. Living quarters for the next generation of Taylors. New thieves, murderers, self-loathing racists, drug dealers, rising up to fill the void left behind by Grandma and her favorite grandson, Oba.

"Most of the Taylor outfit are in town, waiting to claim Oba's body," Kinta points toward a hilltop behind the house, bristling with wooden crosses. Richard sees a fresh rectangular mound of earth by the newest cross—Grandma's final resting place—and an open grave next door that waits for Oba's body.

The soil of the little cemetery is bare and rocky. Erosion gullies tip the crosses and give the hill the texture of a fissured rectum. There is no grass or shrubbery—nothing holds the earth.

"Meanness has poisoned the soil." Once again, Kinta reads Richard's mind. "Won't support vegetation except for a weed or two."

Richard missed the bald hilltop cemetery when he was here before. Too busy looking at Otto's double-barreled shotgun, and Earline Taylor's overactive tongue, and the bloated body on the table, and the stubble on Wolfie Lafleur's shaved head.

"Oba's trailer is the Airstream." Kinta nods her head at the rusty art deco mobile home sitting crooked on cinder blocks. Richard wonders how she knows. Starts to ask but another flash of light in the cedar trees interrupts his train of thought. He wants to get this quest over with before the people in the forest get less curious and more aggressive.

The pit bulls vanish when Kinta's bacon is all gone. They separate and disappear among the trailers and trash piles that scar the Taylor clearing like a bad case of acne. Oba's Airstream looks abandoned but so do all the other trailers scattered over the uneven terrain. They are tipped and rusted. Broken windows are patched with cardboard and duct tape. Sides are dented and decorated with primitive spray graffiti that reminds Richard of cave paintings.

He expects people to stumble out of the trailers like extras in the latest zombie apocalypse thriller but the only movement he detects is in the trees.

"Where are the dogs?" He holds the door of Oba's trailer open for Kinta, the way Grandma Clementine taught him a gentleman should. When she steps across the threshold he wants to pull her back. He wants to call the whole thing off, but she's inside before he can think of a way to do it without sounding like a coward. So he follows her, the way he has been following Kinta since he first watched her disappear into the woods behind his house. The air is stale and dry inside the Airstream. Its rounded roof looks organic, like a birth canal that will spit him out into a new world he knows nothing about. It's not as dark as he expected.

He pulls back the curtains, mostly because he doesn't know what else to do. They rip in his hands and fill the room with dust motes that spin through the inside of the trailer like the Andromeda Galaxy.

Furniture is sparse. Not much more inviting than the inside of a prison cell. The odor of rodent urine makes Richard's eyes water; Kinta doesn't seem to notice.

There's a single bed that's probably been unmade since Oba was arrested. There's a bedside stand made of laminated wood. Kinta pulls the top drawer open.

"Pornography," she lifts magazines out one by one and stacks them on the bed. *Hogtied Bitches* is the most popular, but there are also a few issues of *Stand Corrected*, and *The Corporal Digest*.

Richard brushes his fingers over the top magazine, the way a blind man reads brail. Tries to understand why these things are erotic. Can't make sense of it, but they most definitely are.

He blushes when Kinta stops what she's doing and looks at him. He's seen that expression on a woman's face before, when a mother checks her baby's diaper to see if it is soiled.

"Sorry." He doesn't say what he's sorry for. Doesn't know exactly, but he knows the apology goes Old Testament deep. Richard stutters as he tries to roll an explanation off of his tongue. He pulls his hand off of the magazine and wipes it on his shirt.

For the moment the only word he can say is, "Oba." The man who died earlier today while Richard watched and his family tried to save him. The man whose dirty secrets are stacked up on his unmade bed and are not so much different from secrets every man has hidden in a mental pornography drawer. Even holy men, who should know better but can't help themselves because of basic flaws in the manufacturing process.

Kinta continues sorting through the drawer. She puts a gun catalogue on top of the porn magazines. And then a Bible.

"Gideon Bible," she says. "Probably stolen from a hotel."

Richard starts to touch the Bible, but doesn't want to do it with the same hand that brushed across *Hogtied Bitches*.

"I'll search inside the trailer," Kinta tells him. "You look underneath."

"Wolfie Lafleur's gun," Richard says. This is the first time he's mentioned what they are looking for, but somehow Kinta already knows. He'd ask her about it if they weren't searching a dead man's trailer in the Patch with gunmen roaming the woods. If she hadn't seen him touch Oba Taylor's magazine and silently accepted his apology.

The trailer door is still open, letting new air mix with the old. Letting dust from the torn curtains mix with dust from the hilltop graveyard and settle on the Bible and the gun catalogue and the pornography magazines.

Richard stumbles as he steps out the door and falls to the ground beside a void in the cinder blocks holding up the trailer. This must be the place. He crawls through the spider webs, over rotted two-by-fours and broken bricks into the underpinnings of Oba Taylor's former life. Rubber hoses and insulated wires droop into the space. Fingers of sunlight poke through chinks in the foundation and highlight beer bottles, empty Vienna Sausage cans, and the skeleton of a cat.

It's much more complicated underneath the trailer than Richard Harjo imagined. The texture of the earth, the spider webs, the beams of light, and the scattered trash combine with his anxiety to create a landscape where Wolfie Burdette's pistol could hide forever.

Richard wriggles on his belly like a creature working his way down the evolutionary chain. Kinta's footsteps move on the floor above him, much louder than he expected. He takes comfort in the noise she makes. His eyes scan the ground inch by inch while his ears keep track of Kinta's search. She scoots furniture, empties drawers, pushes dishes aside while he tries to remember what he's looking for.

He sees a pair of shadows move along the cinderblock wall toward the front door. Shoes drag across the ground. The smell of cigarette smoke cuts through the odor of organic decay.

He hears Anton Leemaster ask, "Where's your boyfriend?"

"I knew you'd be here sooner or later," Kinta says from the part of the Airstream that doubles as a kitchen / dining room. She takes two steps in Leemaster's direction. The trailer squeaks and shakes on its cinderblock footings. A couple of blocks fall away so Richard can see Anton Leemaster's legs. Close to the doorway. Close enough to leap inside and grab Kinta if he wants to.

And he wants to. Richard can see the nervous movements in his legs. A foot moves forward, then back. All the weight is on the toes like a Latin dance.

"It's been a long time since we've been this close together," Anton says. "A real long time. Why don't I come inside?"

Richard crawls toward the voices, salamander style. Careless of the bricks and boards and bottles. Careless of the spiders.

"Nobody important is watching us," Anton says. "Just a few of Oba's kin scattered in the woods."

The trailer shifts as Kinta steps back and Anton Leemaster steps inside. The mobile home's aluminum skin strains against the frame. It pops and creaks like a worn out innerspring mattress in a motel room that's rented by the hour. The noises blend perfectly with the scuffs and scrapes of Richard's progress across the crawl space.

He is breathing hard, moaning, cursing Anton Leemaster under his breath. He's almost made it to the missing blocks where he came in when the palm of his hand pushes against the metal box partially covered by debris.

"What's the matter?" Anton Leemaster's voice is full of authority, like a man who's accustomed to strapping killers onto an execution table.

Richard takes some time to consider what he might do when he crawls out from under the trailer.

"Not afraid of me, are you?" The rhythm of Anton Leemaster's words is like the background music in a slasher film. Ugly, dangerous, unambiguous.

Richard finds the catch on the metal box, flips it open. Inside is Wolfie Burdette's gun, wrapped in an oily rag.

32

The pistol is a big black collection of rectangles. Lots of plastic. What metal there is has a matte finish that won't hold fingerprints or support rust. It might be a nine millimeter, or a thirty-eight caliber, or even a forty-five. Richard has no idea, but the hole at the end of the barrel is as big as the tip of his trigger finger and his hand feels power in the grip as he holds the weapon in the killing position and crawls into the late afternoon sunlight of the Patch.

He feels really witchy as he stands in front of the Airstream door and holds the pistol in the shooter's stance he's seen television cops assume. The pistol grip is warm in his hands—a perfect fit—and the frame feels lighter than air. He wants to say something to Anton Leemaster. Something powerful and scary like, "let me see your hands, asshole," so Kinta and the prison guard will immediately see how things are going to play out.

But Richard remembers things like safety catches and how some pistols have them and some pistols don't. He remembers clips and bullets and "jacking one into the spout," whatever that means, and he's not really sure what will happen when he pulls the trigger.

Kinta smiles at Richard over Anton Leemaster's shoulder. Nods her head, which he takes to mean, "Now's the time to shoot."

"Why are you smiling?" Leemaster asks her, but he doesn't turn around to see what she is looking at. There's no mistaking the sound of fear in the guard's voice. The pitch, the slight vibrato, the way he clears his throat after he asks his question.

Richard doesn't know if the pistol will fire when he pulls the trigger. If it does, will the bullet pass through Leemaster and kill Kinta? If it doesn't, has Leemaster brought a gun? How much time will Richard have to figure things out and take his shot?

A lot of things to think about for a preacher pointing a loaded gun at a human being for the first time in his life. Getting ready to see what it's like to break commandment number six, which falls between honoring your parents and committing adultery.

"Goddamn it." Richard decides to start with commandment number three and see where things go from there.

"Turn around, Leemaster. I want to look into your eyes when you see it coming." Richard thinks Clint Eastwood may have said that—in a Dirty Harry movie or a spaghetti western. It's not as loud as a gunshot but it makes his point.

A man with long hair steps out of the cedar trees at the edge of the clearing. Then a man with no hair at all. Richard thinks the second man might be Wolfie Lafleur, but he's too far away to know for sure.

Two more men step out of the trees, and a woman, Richard thinks is Earline Taylor.

"Shoot," Kinta tells him. Anton Leemaster is trying to keep an eye on Kinta and look behind him at the same time. He jerks his head back and forth the way meth addicts do when their drug reaches its circulatory-system peak.

"Chicken head movements," Richard says. He closes his left eye and sights down the barrel of the pistol. He pushes the tip of his tongue between his lips and then pulls it back inside because he knows he might involuntarily clench when the gun discharges in his hand and showers Kinta and Oba Taylor's trailer with specks of Anton Leemaster's blood.

He aims for the center of Leemaster's back because that's the largest target. "Step away, Kinta." But when Kinta steps away he still doesn't pull the trigger.

Anton Leemaster turns and faces Richard Harjo. Otto's name is written in big inflamed name-belt letters across his face. He holds the palms of his hands forward but doesn't raise them past his shoulders.

Richard feels the pistol gaining weight in his hands, feels the oily moisture in his palms lubricate the plastic grip. Tries to think of more quotes from Clint Eastwood to fill up the next few moments while he convinces his trigger finger to follow orders.

More Taylor friends and relatives emerge from the woods. Patch residents who took cover in the trees when the witch couple strolled into town with their entourage of killer dogs. Now they're moving closer so they can watch the life drain out of Anton Leemaster's eyes when Richard finally kills him.

Anton is still in his guard's uniform. Patch residents all know it by sight. The man who stopped Oba Taylor's heart with a shock stick is going to die right here in front of Oba's Airstream trailer. Not far from his empty grave. And no Taylor kin will get in trouble.

"Ironic," Richard says loud enough for the Patch residents to hear, because they really should know what kind of moment this is.

"Shoot him." Kinta's voice sounds mechanical inside the Airstream.

Richard sees a smirk curl one side of Anton Leemaster's mouth. The guard's hands lower in increments. They move toward his belt, where Richard sees a pistol stuck in the waistband of his pants, the barrel pointed toward his penis.

"Shoot him, Richard." Kinta steps behind Anton Leemaster again. Throws Richard an angry look, which makes him want to pull the trigger a little more than he doesn't want to see a splotch of blood spread across Leemaster's chest.

The equilibrium is broken. Richard's finger tightens on the trigger, which compresses under the force, because this pistol has no safety catch. His hands bounce in anticipation of the explosion—that doesn't happen.

No recoil because there is no bullet "in the spout."

Richard wants to tell Kinta, "I was willing." Wants to tell her how he pulled the trigger and even though nothing happened, his willingness should be worth something. Doesn't want to tell her he's glad the pistol didn't fire because murder is something a doctorate in divinity and a PhD in psychology never prepared him for.

Leemaster's smirk blossoms into a photographic smile as his hands move toward his pistol. Lots of teeth, like the smiles Richard has seen on pictures of former President Jimmy Carter. "Hey there, Rev."

Richard abandons his two-handed shooter's stance long enough to work the ejection slide. He sees a brass cartridge pop into the chamber in slow motion. Sees fingerprint smudges on the brass. Takes note of the copper jacket on the lead dome that will spread out when it hits its target, which Richard understands won't happen because Anton Leemaster is bound to get off the first shot.

The guard pulls the trigger without aiming. Richard sees a disc of fire spread out from the muzzle, and ahead of the flash is a spinning slug that is moving way too fast to see.

Impossible, but Richard sees it anyway.

The slug flies over Richard Harjo's shoulder followed by an explosion that makes his ears ring in a perfect A sharp.

He's temporarily paralyzed by the ringing in his ears and the sudden realization that he is about to die here in the Patch. That his body will be thrown into a grave in the Taylor family cemetery. The man who stole Grandma Angina's tortoise shell hair clips and gave them to her favorite grandson. Perhaps there'll be a wooden cross made of termite-infested two-by-fours scrounged from the lumber skeleton of the Taylor ancestral home.

Richard has time to remember his hand and his father's hand separated by a pane of safety glass, Grandma Clementine telling him bedtime stories that mixed Bible passages with Creek legends, Holabi Minco putting popsicle sticks into his pocket, Kinta wrapping her naked body around his in the middle of the night.

His life races by exactly the way he'd always heard it would, right up to the present. Then things slow down to normal speed. Leemaster takes careful aim because it's clear that Richard is never going to fire a shot. The guard's finger tightens on the trigger.

No time for a rerun of Richard's life. He wonders if he can duck under the slug as the muzzle flares again.

Richard can't see this one. Can't feel the heat from the explosion of nitrocellulose, because Anton Leemaster pitches forward as he shoots.

Kinta has kicked him out the door. The guard drops his weapon as he falls. Catches himself on his hands as he hits the ground.

"Shoot him." Kinta hops out of the trailer. Hits the ground like a gold medal gymnast sticking a perfect landing.

"Shoot him, now." Kinta has a one-track mind.

Richard knows the weapon in his hands has killed at least once—a state trooper who made the mistake giving Wolfie Lafleur the benefit of the doubt. The weapon is experienced and ready, but Richard Harjo isn't. He can't pull the trigger. Not with Anton Leemaster crawling away from him like a wounded animal. No excuses now that he has a bullet in the chamber and knows there is no safety. Witnesses move closer from the woods, but they are witnesses who'll never spread Richard's guilt beyond the Patch.

Richard follows Leemaster with the business end of the weapon hoping a spasm will do the job he can't bring himself to finish. Killing a man without giving him a chance to pray, to sing his death song, to select a last meal from Geraldine's restaurant. That's not how it's done. Richard wonders if he'll be able to shoot when Leemaster finally puts his hand on his pistol, because it's pretty obvious that's what the guard is going for.

Richard squeezes the trigger. Feels the pistol recoil in his hands. The shot kicks up a mushroom cloud of dust beside Anton Leemaster as he reaches his pistol and stands.

The anticipation of a close range gunfight with lots of wild bullets sends Patch witnesses running back into the trees.

Kinta steps between Richard and Leemaster. Slows the guard down with a quick kick to his groin. She has a knife in her hand. Richard recognizes it. The knife Tammy Wynette Biggerstaff used to kill Samantha. The knife Kinta used to stab Burdette Lafleur. Richard thought she left it with Samantha's bones. Something for the police to sort out later on, but here it is.

Kinta swings the knife like an old time cutlass. A clean sharp arc to the side of Anton's face where the word Otto is printed in the color of clotted blood. His ear bounces off of his shoulder and lands on the ground.

Leemaster can't decide which pain deserves the most attention. He staggers back away from his ear, holding the place where it used to be with his pistol-free hand.

"Shoot him, Richard. Go on. Put him out of his misery."

Leemaster is miserable enough that Richard just might do it. The guard runs a broken field path across the clearing. Firing random shots. Staggering from the pain in his groin and the loss of blood from his amputated ear.

Kinta puts two fingers in her mouth and whistles like a fourth of July rocket getting ready to explode.

The three bacon-tamed pit bulls gather around her wagging their tails. Kinta picks up Leemaster's ear, cuts it in three pieces, tosses one to each dog. They swallow their bits of Anton Leemaster whole, then turn and watch him run toward the hilltop cemetery.

"Get him," Kinta tells them.

The dogs don't hesitate the way Richard did. They don't remember their fathers and their grandmothers and the girl they made love to last night. They remember that the bacon is gone and that Anton Leemaster has another ear.

The guard stops to fire a couple of shots at the pit bulls, but they are running too low and moving too fast and he's shaking too much to take aim. Finally he runs to the only spot that offers any safety to a one-eared man with a belt marked face and a bruised groin. Oba Taylor's open grave.

"We'd better head back," Kinta says. "Those dogs will lose interest after a while."

Richard puts Wolfie Lafleur's pistol into his waistband the way Anton Leemaster wore his gun. The metal feels hot against his skin. It burns, but not enough to stop and take it out.

33

Richard wants to ask Kinta why Anton Leemaster is obsessed with her. Did she lead the guard on when he worked visitation?

"Holabi thought he wouldn't need a holy man." Richard wants to ask Kinta what her father meant by that. He wants to ask if she seduced Leemaster first. Bewitched him to get special treatment for her father, and when that didn't go as planned . . . .

Before Richard can work out how to ask the question, she answers with a kiss. And then another kiss. And follows up with things he hadn't thought about since he was sixteen years old. Well maybe he's thought about them from time to time but he filed them away as unrealistic fantasies like Santa Claus, and honest politicians, and girls who like the taste of semen.

When Kinta is finished with Richard, his questions don't seem relevant anymore. What seems relevant is lying beside her in a bed he hadn't realized was far too wide until she came into his life. He can still see her after she turns out the bedroom light, glowing like a Hindu mystic's vision of the Kama Sutra. He can still see her when his eyes are closed.

"Kinta?" he says her name like it's a question, but he knows it's one of those enigmatic questions that don't really have an answer. All his life, Richard has been telling himself that sex is just a biological drive inserted in human DNA by God—or chance—to insure survival of the species. That love is a chemical cascade of neurologically-active hormones designed by God—or natural selection—to cement the family unit.

But as he watches Kinta's glowing face twitch in REM sleep and settle into a perfectly symmetrical smile he realized he had it wrong. Sex—with her at least—is magic. Everything with Kinta Minco is magic.

When sunrise wakens Richard, she is gone. He sorts through his memories trying figure out which parts are real and which are fantasy.

He spends a few minutes looking at the Kinta shaped wrinkles in his sheets. A few more minutes inhaling air that carries her scent. There are floral tones in the odors Kinta left behind, and herbal notes, and subliminal tones that go directly to the pleasure centers in his brain.

"Love." Richard Harjo has fallen in love, the way Grandma Clementine said he would. Grandma talked about true love and puppy love and eternal love and love at first sight. She also talked about witchcraft and seduction and falling under the spell of a pretty girl. Is there really any difference?

At this point it didn't matter. He'd gone to the Patch for Kinta Minco. Been willing to commit class D felonies for her. Been willing to kill for her—although it hadn't worked out that way.

He thanks God silently for that, but he doesn't ask God to forgive him for all the commandments he's broken during the month of August. Women's Month.

"Kinta's month," Richard whispers to the spot on his bed where Kinta had slept. He touches the impression of her body with his hand. Still warm. He thinks that spot will always be warm. Warm in that mysterious witchy way he's learned to expect from Kinta Minco.

He leaves his bed rumpled by last night's activities because disturbing it seems like desecration. He showers even though that seems like desecration too, and walks into the kitchen. There's a pie cooling on the kitchen table, and a note: Dead'n'berried Pie. Don't eat it.

Richard tests the pie's weight. Nothing that can't be accounted for by the flaky crust and the berry filling and the glass pie plate that will allow guards to look at it from every angle and see that it's a harmless thing. As harmless as a mason jar filled with pretend holy water.

He remembers it is Moving Day on H-Unit. When Holabi Minco takes his last shower and dresses in his last prison jump suit and moves into the Waiting Room and prepares himself for execution. At 12:01 a.m. One minute after the witching hour. The Farmer's Almanac promises a full moon with a lunar eclipse. The time was chosen by a judge with Choctaw blood to celebrate the fact that Holabi Minco is a witch as well as a murderer. A show of respect for Minco's power. For his Indian ways. And maybe a chance for a man of power to escape. To turn into an owl and fly away under the magic red light of an eclipsed full moon in full view of the prison guards.

Impossible. No one has ever escaped from H-Unit. Too many guards. Too many double doors, and thanks to Oba Taylor's failed escape attempt, the executioners will put their black hoods and robes on after they enter the prison. After the guards have checked their ID's against a list provided by the warden.

Getting out of H-Unit would be magic, and in spite of everything Richard has seen—and everything he's studied in seminary—he isn't ready to believe in magic. Except for Kinta, naturally. He's perfectly willing to believe in her.

Madeline walks beside Richard to the Waiting Room. Tells him all the guards are worried.

"Anton Leemaster didn't come in this morning. He's always here on Moving Day. Takes the last meal order. Gloats over the execution . . . you know." She's sure he wouldn't miss the chance to harass Holabi Minco one last day. To watch him naked and vulnerable in the shower. To get his last meal order wrong.

"It's not like Anton to miss the opportunity." She stops at the Waiting Room door and lets Richard go in alone. Won't cross the threshold and expose herself to all the ghosts that might be inside holding grudges.

"Lunar eclipse tonight," she reminds him. The moon will fall into the shadow of the earth. It will turn yellow and then red.

"New skin moon," Richard says. Grandma Clementine used to call it that. "The moon loses her old skin and grows a new one when everything's about to change."

"Everything." Madeline looks down the hallway at the sound of shackles, rattling and echoing along the cement hallway of H-Unit.

Holabi Minco is one of those things that is about to change. He's accompanied by four guards, like Oba, even though he's never shown the slightest violent tendency. The guards are Native American men, assigned by a prison administration that classifies Native American mysticism as superstition but acknowledges it anyway. The four guards stand away from Holabi, holding their shock sticks. Their eyes are filled with terror and respect. They believe Minco witched Anton Leemaster from his prison cell.

Richard wonders if the Indian guards have got it right. Maybe Minco has been witching everyone since he was sent to H-Unit three years ago. How many times has the moon changed her skin since then?

"How witchy do you feel today?" Holabi asks as he walks into the Waiting Room. The guards stand outside the cell while Madeline removes his shackles. She winds the chains in neat, loose loops around one arm. Tells Holabi, "Sorry about the restraints."

The Indian guards know chains are no defense against magic. Neither are shock sticks, but they grip them harder than ever because they are standing outside the final cell of a murdering Choctaw witch and a Creek chaplain who somehow killed an inmate with Hail Marys and holy water.

They look around the floor for owl feathers while Madeline asks Holabi what he wants for his last meal.

"Anton usually takes the orders, but since he's gone . . . ." She doesn't recommend Chicken Fried Steak and Okra from Geraldine's. She doesn't have a clipboard with a yellow pad to write things down, because no one will forget a Choctaw witch's last meal order. No one would dare to get it wrong.

"I want a double stick orange popsicle," Holabi tells her. "And a big slice of Dead'n'berried Pie."

Richard watches Madeline's lips move. Sees the question in her eyes. Holabi isn't looking at her but he senses it too.

"It's traditional, Madeline. You bring the popsicle. The Rev will take care of the rest."

Holabi hands Richard the Waiting Room Bible. "Open it. Mathew 10:28."

The verse is underlined in a shaky reddish brown line that once was the color of the names Holabi Minco wrote on popsicle sticks. Blood, but older blood, brown and reticulated by time.

Richard knows the verse but in the context of blood it means something different: "And do not fear those who kill the body but cannot kill the soul."

"Look at the bottom of the page, Rev."

Richard Harjo reads his own name written in old blood underneath the passages. Nervous block letters smeared but legible. The name is repeated backwards on the opposite page. A faded mirror transfer of Richard's name. His father's name, written in the Waiting Room Bible the day before the state of Oklahoma executed him.

Madeline steps into the cell and reads the blood message over Richard's shoulder.

"What's it mean, Holabi?" she asks.

"Probably don't mean nothing, but it's mysterious as hell."

Holabi takes the Bible from Richard's hands. Closes it and hands it back.

"Take it home with you, Rev. "That signature makes this your family Bible."

34

The execution witness list is a closely held secret. The condemned man is permitted three invitations. The state has three, and the victims' relatives and friends share the remaining six with journalists. Twelve chairs—like the twelve chairs in a jury box—behind reinforced safety glass that remains curtained until it's certain the governor won't call. Then the curtains jerk back with a pop that brings everybody into the present. The condemned inmate fumbles through his last words and the hooded executioners push the buttons in their hidden cubicle.

The first two guards Richard Harjo meets on his way into the prison tell him things aren't going to happen like that tonight. "No witnesses, Rev. No victim's relatives. Not even any press."

The prison couldn't recruit local executioners. "Brought white men all the way from Oklahoma City, Rev. That's the rumor anyway." The guards talk to him through a cheap speaker behind the glass security wall of the first set of double doors Richard has to pass to get to H-Unit. They don't ask to see the pie he's carrying. They don't ask him about Kinta Minco, who kissed him at the entrance and then disappeared into the darkness like an evil spirit.

Richard holds the pie so the guards can see it. They can confiscate it if they choose. A part of him hopes they will, because he knows Kinta didn't bake this pie so her death row inmate father could die with the taste of berries in his mouth.

The guards at the other security intersections pass him through with a wave and a nod until he reaches the last one. Only one guard behind that window. Blond hair, blue eyes. A complete absence of tribal blood. His voice is filled with ignorance and curiosity when he asks, "Who'd Minco murder anyways, Rev? You know the story?"

The kind of curiosity that's been killing cats since the dawn of time. Prisons are saturated with rumors. Every inmate has a story and plenty of time to tell it. Every guard, every nurse, every PA, dentist, doctor, administrator, has heard them a thousand times, but no one admits any knowledge of Holabi Minco's crimes. Only that he killed someone. Probably lots of someones. Only that no bodies were ever found. His record is available, but no prison employee wants to touch a piece of paper with a witch's name written on it.

Richard tips the pie so the guard behind the window can watch Dead'n'berried juice seep through perforations in the crust. Knife perforations. Richard examines the pie's reflection in the bulletproof glass between him and the guard. The perforations are exact width of the knife Tammy Biggerstaff used to kill her lover. The knife Kinta used to stab Burdette Lafleur and amputate Anton Leemaster's ear. The berry juice is the color of human blood. No flies have disturbed it even though it is August and the summer air is full of them.

"Dead'nberried pie," Richard tells the guard. "Holabi's last meal. There's plenty if you want to try a piece."

The guard keeps his eyes on the seeping red berry juice while the final door slides open and allows Richard to walk into the rarified air of H-Unit four hours before Holabi Minco's scheduled execution, where Madeline is waiting to walk him to the Waiting Room.

A dozen cell doors alternate with blank spaces in the hall all the way to the death chamber. They are staggered, so when an inmate looks through his viewing window, all he sees is a cement wall. All the doors are locked except for the bright yellow one a few feet from the execution room.

The Waiting Room door is open, the way it was for Tammy Wynette Biggerstaff. The way it wasn't for Oba Taylor.

"Out of respect," Madeline tells Richard. The guards are afraid of Holabi Minco but in a different way than they were afraid of Oba Taylor.

Two male guards stand on each side of the open door, gripping their shock sticks, looking uneasy. Holabi Minco's voice echoes down the hall, bouncing a Choctaw chant off of the concrete surfaces. Too discordant to be called music. Too high pitched to be a prayer.

"Death song," Madeline tells Richard. "He's been going at it ever since you left."

"Not exactly a toe-tapper, is it, Rev?" Holabi looks happy enough for a man who's about to die. "Got to set the mood, you know, for when they walk me down the mile."

He doesn't ask what time it is, like every other occupant of the Waiting Room. Holabi's eyes go straight to the Dead'n'berried pie.

"Don't suppose I could get a knife and fork?"

Madeline hands him plastic cutlery set along with a napkin. "No metal. Prison rules." As if it isn't breaking prison rules to bring in Kinta's pie.

She looks at the glass pie pan. "Don't do nothin' crazy, Holabi." The four guards in the hallway fidget around the open door like children who've been called to the principal's office and have heard rumors of a paddling machine.

"Boo!" Holabi lunges toward them. Sends the guards stumbling over each other to get away. They regroup quickly and charge the door—but they don't cross the threshold. Only Madeline will go that far, and only because she must.

One of them says, "We're watching you, Minco." His voice cracks mid-sentence. He tries to stare Holabi Minco down but loses the contest by the count of five.

"Want to join me for some pie, boys?" He tips the pie so Dead'n'berried juice runs out the perforations and drips off the crust onto the prison floor. Madeline tries to soak it up with a napkin but the stain has already set into the gunite, a permanent mark on the Waiting Room left by the Choctaw witch executed during a lunar eclipse, if everything goes according to schedule.

Richard thinks it won't. Holabi and Kinta have something planned. Richard figures he's a crucial part of it even if he doesn't know exactly how. The devil—as they say—is in the details, and Richard is starting to believe in the devil now.

"How 'bout my popsicle, Madeline?" Holabi points to Richard's watch. "Time's wastin'. Ain't that right, Rev."

Richard looks at his watch. Time is definitely wasting. He watches the minute hand jump to the next number.

"Anton is still missing." Madeline looks at Richard. Then at Holabi Minco. When neither one speaks she walks backward out the door.

Appetite is something most men lose when they are about to die. Holabi is different. "Ain't nothin' to be afraid of, Rev. You held Tammy's hand all the way to the end of the tunnel, didn't you? Saw there was something on the other side."

"That's more than most holy men know for sure." He bites into the popsicle, swallows the mushy orange ice fast enough to get a brain freeze, smiles through the pain. "Last headache I'll ever have. Might as well enjoy it." He tosses one of the sticks into his plastic trashcan, licks the juice off of the other one and hands it to Richard.

"Something you need to do, Rev." He reaches into a pocket of his DOC jump suit and pulls out an owl feather. The male guards outside his cell watch him, but Madeline's eyes are fixed on the Dead'n'berried pie.

Holabi sharpens his plastic knife on the gunite floor, quickly and efficiently as a man who's accustomed to making shanks on short notice. He tests the edge on his thumb and then whittles the quill of the feather into a point.

"In H-Unit, everything's forbidden. Anything is possible." He inspects his work. Finds it satisfactory.

When Holabi Minco dips the pointed end of the owl feather into Dead'n'berried juice, Richard understands the witch has made an old-fashioned quill pen.

"Here you go." He hands the dripping quill pen to Richard. "You know what to do by now. Don't you, Rev?"

Richard is surprised to find he knows exactly what to do. He writes Minco's name on his popsicle stick. Not in blood. Nobody but a real witch would do that, but when Richard Harjo dots the I's in Holabi Minco's name he's feeling pretty witchy.

"An educated man is too smart to believe in something he can't see." Richard Harjo was twelve years old when Grandma told him that.

"Too smart to believe he's got a soul until he trades it for a handful of magic beans." Grandma Clementine's wisdom has come back to him many times during the month of August. He doesn't usually share it.

"I don't believe in magic beans," Richard says "But magic popsicle sticks?" Has he traded his soul for one of those?

Holabi cuts a triangular piece of pie with his razor sharp plastic cutlery shank and eats it in four bites. "Wish I had a beer to go with this."

He's half way through his second piece when Madeline tells him, "I can get you a soda pop, but alcohol's illegal."

"Guess I'd better have a Mountain Dew, then. I'm in enough trouble as it is." Holabi follows that statement with some words Richard can't understand. They might be magic Choctaw words, or ordinary English stretched around a giant mouthful of Dead'n'berried pie.

35

Richard has an owl feather quill pen in one hand and a popsicle stick in the other and can't decide what to do with either.

"Probably don't matter," Madeline tells him. "The magic is done once his name's on the calendar."

He tries to hand the popsicle stick and the owl feather pen to Madeline but she pulls away. She back-steps out of the Waiting Room. Raises her right hand and imitates a three fingered Girl Scout half-salute.

Holabi swallows another mouthful of pie, says, "Chi pisa la chika," and waves to her.

"Means see you later," Madeline tells Richard. She backs against the blank wall opposite the waiting room door. Pushes herself against it as if she's standing on a narrow ledge. she turns her attention to the final security door between the outside world and the twelve cells of H-Unit's death row. "Anton!"

Richard steps out of the cell as the sliding door opens and Anton Leemaster lurches into the hallway, blood on his face, blood in his hair, blood oozing from the place where his ear used to be. He stumbles down the hall like a monster in a grade B horror movie. Appropriate. The last time Richard saw Anton Leemaster he was at the bottom of an open grave surrounded by angry pit bulls.

Three Hooded Men follow Anton. Hanging back. Fearful of the one-eared prison guard with the dirty uniform and the bloody face with Otto printed across it.

"That son of a bitch can't die without me bein' here," Anton Leemaster points a grimy finger at the open door of the Waiting Room. He swipes his hand over his missing ear and starts it bleeding again. A lot of blood. Enough blood to fill a transfusion bag and then some.

The executioners from Oklahoma City expected to be the terrifying apparitions in the death row hallway, but they are hopelessly outclassed by Anton Leemaster. The three men huddle together like a bouquet of black flowers and watch the horror show through the eyeholes in their hoods.

"You need to see the doctor." Madeline states the obvious, but at least she's saying something. Richard tries to summon up some good advice. Something from the ministry or something from his psychology training, something Grandma Clementine told him when he was a boy, but all he can think of are the owl feather pen and the popsicle stick in his hands. Especially now that Anton Leemaster has noticed them.

The guard reaches into his waistband where he kept his pistol earlier today, but it isn't there. The pistol is gone, like Leemaster's ear and his sanity.

The three Hooded Men whisper to each other and point at the bloody, filthy guard. This is their first time working the execution circuit. Their first brush with Indian Magic. It's not as entertaining as they imagined. Richard watches their eyes bounce around behind the eyeholes in their hoods. Looking for some kind of sense in the cement hallway, but all they see is a madman without an ear, and five prison guards in crisp clean uniforms, and a man who is none of those things holding an owl feather in one hand and a popsicle stick in the other.

It's almost enough to send them scampering back to the security doors, but they are frozen to the spot when Holabi Minco steps into the hallway.

He gives Anton Leemaster a little salute and then eases himself onto the floor, lies flat and begins an elaborate grand mal seizure that begins in his hands and spreads like an electric current through his body. His arms and legs flutter like a child making a snow angel. His mouth fills to the top with red foam and then runs over. A wet circle forms in the crotch of his jumpsuit. His seizure comes to a sudden stop, as if someone pushed the pause button on a cosmic DVR.

Anton crouches beside Holabi Minco. Feels for a pulse in his neck. The guard's ear wound opens up again and covers Minco's face with blood. It is exactly the same color as the Dead'n'berried foam.

Richard drops his owl feather and his popsicle stick on the floor beside Holabi. "Guess the state won't execute him after all." He hadn't thought that would be Minco's plan. To escape execution by suicide. To sneak out of the prison through the tunnel that leads straight to the afterlife. To dig his escape route through a Dead'n'berried pie with a plastic knife and fork.

The Hooded Men crowd in a tight triangle around Leemaster and Holabi. One asks, "Do we still get the hundred dollars?"

Anton Leemaster picks up the popsicle stick. Reads Holabi Minco's name and drops it again.

"She won't want you," he tells Richard. "Now that you've been part of this."

Richard is the only one who notices when the execution tech arrives. A new one. It's always a new one. This tech is white and young. The fresh look on his face turns sour as he sees the bloody mess on the floor. He pushes his way through the Hooded Men. Checks Holabi's pulse. Watches his chest for signs of breathing. "No pulse or respiration. Way too messy for CPR."

He talks into his headset to someone with the authority to pronounce the inmate dead. He checks his watch. "12:01 a.m., right on time."

According to Richard's watch it's 11:15 p.m. but he doesn't contradict the tech. Something about this execution has to look right on paper.

"Guess we're done here," the technician says. "Let's bag him and transport him."

He doesn't argue when the one-eared bloody guard says, "I'll take care of that."

36

"Nobody checked to see if the Governor called." Richard doesn't usually walk the body of an executed inmate to the morgue van in the parking lot, but there's nothing usual about this execution.

Madeline walks on one side of Minco's gurney. Anton walks on the other. Richard follows, waiting to see what happens when he meets Kinta in the employee parking lot and tells her what happened with her father and her Dead'n'berried pie. Will she want him after that? Probably not, but she won't want a one-eared crazy prison guard who tried to shoot her either. He's pretty sure things won't work out the way Anton Leemaster hopes.

The plastic bag with Minco inside it has settled on the inmate's face. It's an image that's too horrid to walk beside so Madeline tents it up. She smoothes the wrinkles into the excess plastic under Minco's chin.

"Pissed his pants at the end," Anton says. "The way they always do." As if that's some kind of personal victory for the guard. As if it proves Minco never had any power after all.

"Minco loses this one." Anton swaggers beside the gurney for a few steps but he switches to a normal walk when his ear starts oozing blood again.

"You lose too, Rev. Cowboys beat the Injuns every time." The security doors open as they approach and close after they pass. Perfectly timed. No reason to slow the funeral procession down after so much has gone wrong.

"Women always go with the winners," Anton says. "Especially since I didn't have nothing to do with her old man's dyin.'" He looks over his shoulder at Richard.

"They'll cut him to pieces in the morgue you know." Anton is the first to step into the pink light of the lunar eclipse. He holds up a hand like a traffic cop, stops Richard and Madeline and what's left of Holabi Minco halfway through the door.

"New skin moon." Richard quotes Grandma Clementine. The trees around the parking lot are black with pink tops. Their trunks are hidden in shadows as dense and black as the night sky between the stars.

Anton limps to the morgue van, looks in the driver's window. "Nobody home." He opens the back. Checks inside, in case there is something a dead Choctaw witch could use against him. Because anything is possible during a lunar eclipse at midnight during Woman's Month, after an execution that took a witchy turn. He limps off the parking lot, into the shadows of the cedar trees. When he returns his pistol is in his waistband again.

"Can't be too careful." He motions for Madeline and Richard to roll the gurney forward.

They slide Holabi off the slick stainless steel gurney into the van without resistance. A thump, followed by a hissing sound as an air pocket is forced through the zipper, and the plastic settles over the cadaver.

Richard's attention is drawn away from the van by the sound of Kinta's footsteps.

She puts a hand on his shoulder. Puts her arms around him. Kisses him. Exhales in his face and watches him breath in the air that's been inside her. None of Kinta is wasted. None of her left unappreciated, even molecules of August air.

"How witchy do you feel?" she says.

Richard watches the double reflection of the lunar eclipse in her eyes. Her teeth glow luminescent pink in the magic light of the New Skin Moon. It takes him a few seconds to notice the weight of a pistol she's put in his right hand. The grip feels warm and familiar. Its metal is full of heat from Kinta's body. She kisses him again and eases backward across the parking lot as smoothly as if she's being pulled across a sheet of ice.

"He killed your daddy," Anton Leemaster pulls his pistol. Points it half way between Kinta and Richard.

Richard steps away from the van. Three paces, nearly quick enough to make Anton pull the trigger. Plenty quick enough to pull all of his attention away from Kinta.

"Wolfie," Kinta calls from the edge of the parking lot. "Wolfie Lafleur."

Anton Leemaster's pistol jerks toward Kinta and then back to Richard. Like a compass needle that's been confused by a lightning strike.

Richard points his weapon at Leemaster's chest. He steps further from the van. So does the guard. Like a couple of vampire cowboys lining up for a midnight shootout. Things are in motion now. They will stay in motion until everything is finished.

"Anton. You don't have to do this." He knows that isn't true. Anton Leemaster can no more stop himself than a caterpillar can stop itself from becoming a butterfly.

Anton fires a wide shot at Richard. It goes past him and scars the bulletproof glass entryway of the prison. He turns the pistol toward Kinta's voice that's repeating Wolfie Lafleur's name.

A flock of crows flushes from the underbrush at the edge of the parking lot. Anton Leemaster fires his pistol once again.

Richard's vision is already spotted by the yellow after image of the last muzzle flash. Now there are two of them, but he can still see Leemaster. He can still make him out, taking aim. Getting ready to fire again.

Richard Harjo pulls the trigger before that can happen. Hopes it's not too late.

Anton kneels on a yellow line that marks the border of a parking space. He fires a shot into the line and collapses face down on it.

Richard runs across the lot to the last place he saw Kinta standing. Sees a body leaking a black pool of blood onto the tarmac. The New Skin Moon is reflected in the center of the pool. It goes from pink to silver as he watches.

Pristine moonlight illuminates the body. Not Kinta. She steps out of the trees and takes the pistol from Richard's hand. She wipes it clean with the hem of her blouse, rolls the dead man over.

"Wolfie Lafleur." She puts the pistol in his hand and fires a shot at the man in the moon.

"Gunshot residue," she says. "Men like Wolfie usually have a little on their hands, but it pays to be sure."

"I've got to go now," Kinta says. "Don't want to be around when the strike team comes." She smiles as she backs away from Richard, until she disappears into a shadow at the edge of the parking lot.

"Chi pisa la chika," Kinta speaks in Choctaw, so Richard will know what she says is true. "See you later," she translates in case he's forgotten.

As if he could forget anything that happened tonight. Richard walks back toward the van. Toward the only man he's ever killed—unless he counts Lorado Mendez's holy water drowning or Holabi Minco's poisoning.

A strike team moves out the door dressed in riot gear, holding shotguns, ready to shoot someone under the last full moon of Women's Month.

"The killing is already done." Richard holds his hands high and walks toward them as they swarm the truck. Everybody knows him, even in the moonlight. The Creek preacher who killed a Choctaw witch with a popsicle stick.

They kick Anton Leemaster's gun aside and check his pulse.

Two of them go through the morgue truck while three more spread across the parking lot.

"What happened here, Rev?" A strike-team member has pulled Holabi Minco's body bag onto the parking lot. Only Holabi's body isn't in it. What's in it is a handful of owl feathers and a little blood.

Richard doesn't answer because he can't think of anything to say.

"One down over here." Another strike-team member has found Wolfie Lafleur.

Voices on portable police radios fill the parking lot, as the forensic team joins the strike team and they piece together the story of the gunfight on the prison employee parking lot.

"You okay, Rev.? How're you feeling?"

Richard looks for a nametag on the strike-team uniform. There is one, but he can't read it in the moonlight. He makes a silent pledge to start learning everybody's name.

"I guess I feel like a real live holy man." He looks at the moon, then the empty body bag.

"It's not exactly like I thought it would be."

About John T. Biggs

Way back in 1975 I learned that Oklahoma had just opened a new dental school, so I flew in from a U.S. Public Health Service assignment in Maine looking for a job. I expected to find a depressing place with lots of downcast people wishing they had enough gas in their pickup trucks to make it all the way to California—or at least as far as Texas. If I got the job, I figured it would be a start in academics but I probably wouldn't want to stick around.

The state turned out to be nothing like I imagined.

For one thing, Oklahoma Native Americans don't look or act anything like the ones I watched in western movies as a child. There are no pure-blooded tribal members. Perhaps there never really were. Choctaw, Cherokee, Chickasaw, Seminole, Creek, European, African, Jewish, Asian, Middle Eastern and Hispanic are blended together into a very special kind of human being. The Native Americans have moved on in the last hundred plus years, and everybody else has moved on with them.

Okies are a work in progress.

You're allowed to call us that. We're easygoing people with a unique brand of humor, music, and philosophy. We have Oklahoma literature too.

The world is a fascinating place when you look at it from an Oklahoma point of view. Give it a try.

Biography: Why would anybody care where I was born or where I went to school? If you do, here is the short version.

Born: December 8, 1947 in Herrin, Illinois

Parents: Elizabeth and Lowell Biggs. I'm an only child. If you know me, it's easy to figure out why.

Real Biography: People are more complicated than dates and locations. I'm a card-carrying human being and hope to remain one for some time to come. Here's a synopsis of my life.

My Parents

My mother was a hairdresser, freshly divorced from her first husband when she met my dad. People didn't do things like that in the 1940's. Men looked at divorced women with the same suspicion they harbored when shopping for used cars.

There were lots of men looking for wives when she was looking for a husband. Soldiers were coming back to the United States after winning the second world war, full of post traumatic stress disorder—though the disorder had yet to earn that name.

Returning soldiers were in a hurry to marry good old-fashioned American girls and start having lots of babies to make up for all the lives lost fighting the Germans and the Japanese. Master Sergeant Lowell D. Biggs was one of them.

A friend set him up on a blind date with my future mom (his future wife), but he wanted to make sure she was pretty enough before he actually accepted. They didn't have Facebook in those days so he conducted surveillance the way he learned in Italy and North Africa. He hid in the bushes outside her beauty shop and watched her through the windows. It probably wasn't the smartest way to go looking for a girlfriend but it worked.

Dad had a failed marriage under his belt too, so my mother's divorce wasn't a real issue. I guess my parents were ahead of their time when it came to the "till death do us part" section of the marriage vows, at least the first time around. My mother and he dated for two weeks and then got married—the sort of thing Brittany Spears and Kim Kardashian would do much later on.

Lots of people had whirlwind courtships after the war. The men had become acquainted with their own mortality and the women were listening to the ticking of their biological clocks. I was born a year after my parents were married, Dec. 8, 1947, part of the first wave of the Post War Baby Boom Generation.

My dad said to me, "When your mom told me she was pregnant, I thought it was the end of the world."

"Loved you right off when I heard you cry," he said. "Since then, I guess I've been pretty happy."

Well, that might be so, but I'm an only child.

So There I Was In Southern Illinois
Practically all the men were coal miners where I grew up. Southern Illinois was a weird little section of the USA. More in tune with the south than you'd imagine in the state where Abraham Lincoln got his start. People call that part of Illinois the foothills of the Ozarks. It's nothing like the flat fertile farmlands of the central part of the state or the booming metropolis of Chicago.

Unemployment was a way of life. The men worked when the mines weren't on strike and the women mostly stayed home and raised their children. My dad's stepfather decided to break out of the economic cycle and buy a piece of land with proven coal. He set out to compete with Peabody Coal Company with nothing but a positive attitude and a shaky line of credit. It worked out about the way you would imagine.

He signed the mine over to my father and my dad's half-brother about the time a flash flood filled the pit, drowned the equipment, and floated them all downriver to bankruptcy. If you think a bunch of angry coal miners will buy the, "checkbook's under thirty feet of water" excuse, I'm here to tell you they will not.

My mother had a positive attitude. She borrowed $7,000 from her family and bought a junkyard. That was during the enlightened fifties (think *Mad Men*) when women were legally permitted to do anything, but nobody expected them to succeed. Against all odds, she did.

Junkyards Are the Coolest Places Ever

You meet the most interesting class of people around a pile of junk. Unemployed miners down on their luck, local minorities down on their luck, mentally and physically handicapped citizens down on their luck. You've probably guessed the one thing they all had in common.

African American customers drove wagons pulled by mules, loaded with scrap iron they salvaged from around town. That was the 1950s right into the early 1960s. The wagons were built on automobile frames and rolled on bald Goodyear tires. A regular steampunk kind of conveyance.

White customers drove pickup trucks loaded full of copper wire (probably stolen from the mines), brass and aluminum from who knows where, and special metals like bronze, titanium, block tin, and mercury.

Most of our clients had occasional brushes with local law enforcement. My mother and father donated money to everyone who ran for sheriff. "For good will," my dad explained. "Keeps their minds on things besides junk yards." It only had to work long enough for him to load his inventory onto a train and ship it to St. Louis.

Many of the characters in my stories come from those junkyard days. Double amputees who walk on stumps. Grown men who think they have supernatural powers. Boys who will chew up razor blades for fifty cents apiece. Women so ugly they make babies cry but carry pistols to keep unwanted lovers at bay. The most colorful people in the world have spent time around Biggs Iron and Metal Works in Marion, Illinois.

How I Found Love in a Graveyard

I fell in love with Margaret Anderson way before I needed to shave. We lived within two blocks of each other, went to the same junior high and high schools, but we never dated until after we graduated high and I realized it was not beyond the realm of possibility. Everybody told me she was a thousand times too good for me (her mother thought it was closer to two thousand), and it was so obviously true I wouldn't ask her out on a date. She was old fashioned enough she wouldn't ask me either, so her sister stepped in.

The sister had a flare for drama (still does, I guess). She pretended to be Margaret, and invited me to a family barbecue at their cabin on the lake. I accepted as soon as I got my breathing under control. Margaret was better looking than I was, smarter, funnier. Her family was better educated than mine. They were more sophisticated, which you'll probably understand wasn't too difficult.

It was a short drive to the cabin but it was long enough for me to use up my entire inventory of sophisticated conversation topics. I knew a couple of Bob Dylan songs, and some interesting facts about people like Carl Jung, and Werner Von Braun. I could pronounce Frederich Neitzche's name flawlessly and recite a complete list of the kings of France (all those Louis make it pretty easy). But by the time we reached our destination I'd already slipped into more familiar territory like how to sort copper wire by diameter, and how much muscatel wine could be purchased for a pound of brass.

Then we pulled up to the cabin, and I saw my future father-in-law cooking hamburgers on a grill while the rest of my future in-laws sat around on tombstones waiting to be fed.

Tombstones! The Anderson family cabin was built in a graveyard.

Margaret had given me no warning. Not one family member jumped off a headstone and said, "I guess this looks pretty weird," or "Bet you can't guess why this was the most economical lot on the lake." Nobody mentioned the five hundred pound Zombie gorilla at the picnic. Not even me.

My first thought was, "I have gotten hooked up with the Adams family."

My second thought was, "Maybe this will work out after all."

I Was Probably the Worst Dental Student Ever

I started dental school at University of Illinois in Chicago in 1968. Some of you will recognize that year and that location as the luckiest break Richard Nixon ever had, the 1968 Chicago democratic convention.

Some people called it anarchy, some called it a police riot. To me, that's just how Chicago was. The trouble didn't stop when the convention ended. There were police barricades, race riots, anti war demonstrations, bombings, shootings.

I lived in a public housing project for most of the first year, right across the street from Cook County Jail. Then I moved to a series of deteriorating suburbs on the outskirts of the ghetto. My house was robbed. My car was stolen twice, once right off of a police impound lot. I contributed marginally to my own support by working part time as night watchman in a steel door company in Cicero, Illinois, and then in an ink factory in a suburb with a name I don't remember.

Things were pretty bad back then, and I decided it was all the fault of the dental school faculty.

I know.

I got all socially aware but was too busy finding myself to look for anything like real answers. I joined demonstrations, passed around petitions, tried to organize a strike or two. I did all kinds of things without first checking out the facts and then was really surprised when they didn't match up to my concept of reality.

The faculty resented it. The nerve of some people.

Well, I finally saw the error of my ways, which sometimes happens when your back is against the wall. I did what I was supposed to be doing all along and graduated.

Some of the faculty turned out to be sort of nice—go figure.

Easternmost Dentist in the United States

For three years I was a Public Health Dentist on the eastern edge of the continent. Lubec, Maine, in case you're interested. Right across the narrows was Campobello Island, New Brunswick, Canada, where FDR was staying when he first contracted polio. It was one of the most beautiful and weirdest places I have ever lived.

Here are some facts about that part of Maine:

The actual <u>easternmost</u> point in the U.S. is called <u>west</u> Quoddy head.

The tides are twenty-five feet high.

Rivers on the coast flow backwards during certain times of the day.

People think you have a southern accent if you come from Illinois.

A sixty-plus year old transvestite with a beard and several missing fingers lived next door to the building where I worked. His hobby was trapping tourists inside his house. It looked a lot like a shop—complete with a sign over the entrance. He'd hide in the shadows and step in front the doorway after they had ventured inside. They had to listen to his life story until he got bored telling it. He had a very high boredom threshold.

A deaf man who could scream but could not talk followed grocery shoppers through the Lubec A&P. He made noises that sounded like a combination of Tarzan yells and feeding time at the zoo. None of the locals paid him the slightest bit of attention, which made newcomers wonder if rumors about LSD flashbacks were actually true.

We had a store in downtown Lubec that kept an inventory of groceries in order to meet a minimal state requirement for selling beer. There were cans of tuna and lobster in that store that were fresh about the time FDR came down with polio. The proprietor wouldn't sell anything except for beer and beer accessories, even if you had a real hankering for antique canned fish.

I got a lot of much needed dental experience in Maine. I also met two friends, Mike and Jeanie Gougler, who have stuck with me through thin and thinner and thinnest, when I was going through changes that would have discouraged almost anyone.

After three years in Lubec, those friends, my wife, and I were ready to move on.

"I'll go anywhere," I told my good friend Mike.

"I think I can find us jobs in Oklahoma," Mike told me.

"Well, almost anywhere," I said. But by then it was too late.

Oklahoma Was Going To Be a Stop Over

My wife and I moved to Oklahoma in 1975. I thought we might spend a few years there and then move on to someplace better. I'm a baby boomer. I grew up believing there's always someplace better.

The state was nothing like I thought it would be and, truth be told, it probably isn't really like I think it is now. I took a job at the OU College of Dentistry as clinical director of something called the TEAM program. Essentially I was teaching dental students how to set up and operate a private practice. That was something I had never done but somehow that didn't bother me—or dental school administration—and, strangely enough, I think I did a pretty good job.

It was a privilege to teach dental students. They were smart, polite, focused on graduating, and they all had that strain of humor outsiders believe was unique to the late great Will Rogers. OU dental students were almost universally easy to teach, quick to grasp concepts, and grateful for my efforts—nothing like I'd heard teaching is supposed to be—and there were no pesky parents around to make my life miserable.

I would have kept that job forever except for one thing. The TEAM program was funded by a grant, and the grant ran out. So I decided to go to graduate school and specialize in endodontics. That's Root Canals for the uninitiated.

People frequently ask me how I decided on that specialty. I used to tell them I came to one day and I was half way through a graduate program, but here's the real reason: It was a skill set I could master and it paid a lot of money.

Simple as that.

There was a two-month gap between my job and my graduate program, and I filled it by doing dentistry in a prison.

I met rapists and murderers, and robbers and car thieves and mixed media criminals. Since I wasn't on the parole board they didn't mind telling me all about their crimes. Those crimes turn up in my stories from time to time, with the names and details changed so the perpetrators' relatives don't hunt me down and kill me.

I met a man who escorted several Sirloin Stockade employees into a walk in freezer and shot them.

I met a man who had been shot in the face with a twenty-two caliber pistol and didn't go to the doctor because, "Those guys report gunshot wounds."

I met a Vietnam Vet who murdered his wife and her lover and was just about to be paroled to Hawaii after serving twelve years.

I met a good-looking young man who was serving time for rape. He was released when I left for graduate school and by the time I returned he had already re-offended numerous times and was resentenced to over 200 years.

Scared Straight was on TV while I worked in the prison. Lifers in a New Jersey penitentiary interacted with juvenile offenders and tried to intimidate them into changing their criminal ways. It made prison look pretty scary.

"Is it that bad in here?" I asked one of the inmate orderlies in the dental / medical facility.

"Well," he said. "You have to take up for yourself, but it ain't nothin' like when my grandpa was inside."

Chicago Was A Lot Like I Remembered

I really thought I would like Chicago the second time around. I was seven years older by the time I went back to grad school. I had two children and no overwhelming social causes. I was way more mature than when I lived in the Windy City the first time. It was a big bustling metropolis second only to NYC. I had to like it, right?

Well . . .

I learned this much about Chicago: It's no city for someone without money.

Northwestern Dental School was a fantastic experience. The faculty was great. The school was great. It was located by the John Hancock Building near the shore of Lake Michigan. But it was still in the city.

The first outline of a human body I ever saw drawn on a sidewalk was one block from Northwestern. Unfortunately my two children were with me at the time. I had just gotten around to explaining the hard-bitten truth about Santa Clause and now this?

By then, my wife and I were pretty sure we didn't want to stay in Chicago. We could have gone practically everywhere. I had the Northeast Regional Board, the Illinois board, the Oklahoma board, and the board of the U.S. Virgin islands, and that extended my licensure possibilities to all the states that had reciprocity agreements.

One day I came home from graduate school singing one of the few songs with lyrics I can retrieve from my music-defective storage system.

Oklahoma. You know we've got the best state song in the whole world. When I opened the door I heard my wife—who can stay on key better than I can—singing refrains from the same song.

We took it as a sign.

We Know We Belong To The Land

That's part of the lyrics to the state song in case you haven't heard.

My wife is a travel agent. We've been through most of Europe, including Russia, a lot of Asia, parts of Africa and the Middle East, a good part of Central America, Canada, Australia, New Zealand, and the Caribbean. I love to travel, but I'd rather come home to Oklahoma than any place in the world.

It was a great place to practice dentistry. It's a great place to write fiction too. Check it out.

John

Made in the USA
San Bernardino, CA
10 March 2015